MORALDO IN THE CITY
and
A JOURNEY WITH ANITA

Federico Fellini

Moraldo in the City and
A Journey with Anita

Edited and Translated by
John C. Stubbs

University of Illinois Press

URBANA AND CHICAGO

Library of Congress Cataloging in Publication Data

Fellini, Federico.
Moraldo in the city ; and, A journey with Anita.
Translation of 2 unfilmed screenplays: Moraldo in citta and Viaggio con Anita.
1. Moving-picture plays. I. Stubbs, John Caldwell. II. Title.
III. Title: Journey with Anita. IV. Title: Viaggio con Anita.
PN1997.3.F44 1983   791.43′75   82-17526
ISBN 0-252-01023-X

CONTENTS

INTRODUCTION

Moraldo in the City (1954) and *A Journey with Anita* (1957) are two screenplays written by Federico Fellini that he did not film.[1] The publication of these screenplays is an extreme act, but a consistent one, in the field of *auteur* criticism. This body of criticism, first articulated by the French writers of *Cahiers du Cinéma*, holds that the best films are generally made by directors or writer-directors who infuse their movies with a highly personal vision. The films of such directors are parts of an evolving corpus of the artist's work. Viewers and critics are interested both in the movies taken individually and in the evolution of the corpus as a whole. The same is true, I think, for the screenplays in this volume. They are of interest as narratives in their own right and also as parts filling out more clearly Fellini's body of work.

The screenplays are from Fellini's early period in the 1950s when he worked in black and white. The films he completed and released in this period are *Variety Lights* (1950), *The White Sheik* (1952), *I Vitelloni* (1953), *La Strada* (1954), *Il Bidone* (1955), and *Nights of Cabiria* (1956). During this period, beginning with *I Vitelloni*, Fellini began to experiment with the "open" form, an episodic structure that Fellini encountered during his apprenticeship working on neorealistic films such as *Rome, Open City* (1945) and *Paisan* (1946) and then adapted to his own needs. In Fellini's hands the form consists of a string of stories-within-the-story and of diverse scenes that create strong moods. The form allows Fellini

---

[1]Two other unfilmed projects by Fellini exist in written form. One is an adaptation of a book by Mario Tupino, entitled *The Free Women of Magliano*, a series of impressions and portraits of insane men and women in an asylum. Fellini wrote a brief film treatment of the work in 1957. This manuscript is not included in the present volume because it has already been published in English by Gilbert Salachas in *Federico Fellini*, trans. Rosalie Siegel (New York: Crown, 1969), 165-70. The other is an original screenplay called *The Voyage of G. Mastorna*, which deals

to do three things at which he is very good: tell short stories in the ten- to twenty-minute range; develop a variety of aspects of his major characters; and create moments of lyric or haunting mood. One could argue that in certain of Fellini's movies, particularly *Satyricon* (1969) or *Casanova* (1976), some of the episodes of the film are more engrossing than the movie as a whole. But Fellini is most successful when each of his episodes makes its point or establishes its mood *and* when the movie as a whole—the sum of the parts—makes its cumulative point or gives us a portrait that seems full, but not repetitive. Such would seem to be the case with early films like *I Vitelloni, La Strada,* and *Nights of Cabiria* and with later ones like *La Dolce Vita* (1960), *8½* (1963), *Juliet of the Spirits* (1965), and *Amarcord* (1974). And such is also the case with *Moraldo in the City* and *A Journey with Anita.* The two screenplays are successful early uses of the open form.

Among the early films, these screenplays have a certain resemblance to those closest to them in time, *La Strada, Il Bidone,* and *Nights of Cabiria.* Each of these films deals with a central character who undergoes a growth and then experiences a conversion or rejuvenation, either spiritual or secular, at the very end of the film. *Moraldo in the City* and *A Journey with Anita* follow this pattern. More important, however, the screenplays seem also to follow from the autobiographical impulse begun somewhat tentatively in *I Vitelloni* and continued with ever increasing vigor in *La Dolce Vita, 8½, A Director's Notebook* (1969), *The Clowns* (1970), *Roma* (1972), *Amarcord,* and *City of Women* (1980). This autobiographical impulse has, indeed, become one of the elements for which Fellini is best known. Thus, in addition to being considered part of Fellini's early work, the screenplays should be seen as part

---

with a fantastic airplane voyage into the realm of death. Fellini began production of this film project in 1967, with Marcello Mastroianni in the role of the protagonist. However, he became dissatisfied with the shape the project was taking, and, when he fell ill that year, he broke off all work on it. The screenplay is not available for inclusion here because Fellini still hopes to make the film and does not want interest in a project dissipated through a publication of the text in advance.

of a drive in Fellini that cuts through chronological periods.

The autobiographical hero is a major, continuing figure in Fellini's works. Fellini usually treats this hero at important transitions in his psychological-social development. He depicts the hero as late child and young adolescent in the process of discovering sex and other more mature concerns in *8½* and *Amarcord*. He shows the hero as late adolescent and young adult trying to achieve adult independence in *I Vitelloni* and *Roma*. And he examines the hero at a midlife stage in *8½*, when the hero realizes he must plan his future roles in life with the fearful knowledge that time is running out and can reflect with painful lucidity on the events of the past that have brought him where he is. Both of the screenplays published here deal with Fellini's autobiographical hero, and they depict him at such points of transition. *Moraldo in the City* is another treatment of the hero's attempt to move into adulthood as in *I Vitelloni* and *Roma*. The handling in the screenplay, however, is Fellini's fullest on the subject. *A Journey with Anita*, like *8½*, portrays the hero at midlife, attempting to reconcile himself with his past and, thereby, to determine his future. The movie *8½* is clearly the richer work in that it deals with the hero's relationship to his art, whereas *A Journey with Anita* does not. Yet the screenplay in its fuller concentration on the hero's relations with his family strikes its own deep resonances.

The screenplays also present versions of the two locations that are extremely important in Fellini's autobiographical films: the city and the provincial town. Each location has certain associations for Fellini, and the reader will find those associations made clearer by these screenplays. Suffice it to say for the moment that the city in *Moraldo in the City* is a proving ground for the young hero and as such bears certain resemblances to the city in *La Dolce Vita* and *Roma*. Further, the provincial town in *A Journey with Anita* offers the sophisticated hero a place where he can find and reexamine the simplicity, the sense of security, and the strongly felt emotions of his childhood and adolescence. This depiction, in turn, is similar to aspects of Fellini's presentation of the provincial town in *I Vitelloni* and *Amarcord*.

On a less theoretical level, we may note that the screenplays provide us with some early draft versions of scenes, situations, and characters that Fellini employs in later films and essays, usually in more polished form. Fellini makes later use of four specific elements from *Moraldo in the City* and of eleven elements from *A Journey with Anita*. These borrowings are discussed in this introductory essay, and, for the reader's convenience, they are also listed in the appendix.

Fellini wrote *Moraldo in the City* in 1954 in collaboration with his two co-writers of the 1950s, Ennio Flaiano and Tullio Pinelli. The screenplay was intended as a sequel to *I Vitelloni*, a financially successful film that won the Silver Lion Prize of Venice in 1953. *I Vitelloni* is a comedy about a group of young men in a provincial town who try to hold onto their adolescent freedom well into their twenties. Three of them, in particular, try to maintain and project overblown images of their self-importance. One of the group, Moraldo, sees through the sham and, at the end of the movie, leaves the provincial town to seek a career as an adult in the city. As we noted earlier, *I Vitelloni* is a film with autobiographical elements. The provincial town is modeled on Fellini's native Rimini, and the character of Moraldo is modeled on Fellini who did, in fact, leave Rimini in 1937 at the age of seventeen to go first to Florence and then eventually to Rome in search of a career. In *I Vitelloni* the autobiographical protagonist does not, however, hold center stage. He is just one of the group, albeit more sensitive and clear-sighted than the others, and he becomes interesting as a character in his own right mainly as he begins to pull away from the group toward the end of the movie. In *Moraldo in the City* Fellini moves the autobiographical hero to the central position for the first time in the Fellini canon and takes up the subject of Moraldo's attempt to assume adult responsibilities in the city. Moraldo himself is changed somewhat in the sequel. He has journalistic aspirations and an interest in art that he did not have in the earlier work. Indeed, there is little direct reference to the earlier work in the sequel.[2] Fellini clearly wished to extend his previous work rather than merely repeat it.

Moraldo in the City seems to have engaged Fellini's deepest interest in 1954 when he was writing it. However, in 1955 he put the screenplay aside to work on *Il Bidone*, his movie about the life of a swindler. The biographer Angelo Solmi suggests that the project of *Il Bidone* appealed to Fellini more than did *Moraldo in the City* because it seemed to offer more opportunity to recreate the kind of lyricism contained in *La Strada*, the film that won Fellini worldwide fame in 1954 and 1955.[3] However, I suggest instead that Fellini may have felt hesitant about going ahead with a film like *Moraldo in the City*, which would have made him the main subject of the film. Although *I Vitelloni* and *La Dolce Vita* contain autobiographical material, it is not really until *8½* in 1963 that Fellini made himself clearly and undisguisedly the subject of a movie. In 1955 he may not have been ready to open his life to inspection in the way *Moraldo in the City* would have done. There is, of course, a tremendous ego risk involved in filming a part of one's life, even when the life is generalized to represent the late adolescent trying to enter adulthood. What one offers as one's most precious secrets may be rejected by viewers as trivial. Furthermore, there is the problem that unflattering treatment of real people who served as models for characters might cause those people pain. Guido, the hero of *8½*, is fully aware of both of these problems, and his awareness seems a part of his difficulty in completing his autobiographical film. The writing of *Moraldo in the City*, then, may have been a step toward the breakthrough Fellini was to achieve with *8½*, but only a step. In 1955 he may not have

---

[2] The chief reference to the earlier work comes in Section XXXIV, when Moraldo's father states that Moraldo's sister, a major character in *I Vitelloni*, is expecting a second child, who will follow the one born in *I Vitelloni*.

[3] Angelo Solmi, *Fellini*, trans. Elizabeth Greenwood (London: Merlin Press, 1967), 118-19.

been prepared for the breakthrough itself. The particular autobiographical situation of the hero in *Moraldo in the City*, although put aside by Fellini, was not abandoned, however. Later, in *Roma*, Fellini returned to the subject of his entry into the city to seek a career and depicted the mixture of exhilaration and trepidation he felt on his first day in Rome.

The autobiographical period covered in the screenplay is the time shortly after Fellini went to Rome in the spring of 1938. Concerning the screenplay, Fellini has written in a letter: "I can tell you that the screenplay draws on my memories of my first years in Rome. Pinelli and Flaiano helped with the construction of the tale, but the episodes, the characters, and the situations were more or less those I experienced and encountered in those distant years."[4] Relatively little has been written by biographers about this period of Fellini's life. Solmi, who is by far the most complete on Fellini's early days, notes that Fellini worked for a few weeks for the newspaper *Il Popolo di Roma* and for a few months for the film magazine *Cinemagazzino*.[5] Additionally, however, Solmi points out that Fellini did achieve a certain amount of job security in 1939, when he got a position with the satirical weekly *Marc' Aurelio*. Fellini submitted cartoons and stories to the magazine regularly. This kind of position, which provided Fellini with a modest amount of money, is, as the reader will see, not granted to Moraldo in the screenplay.

In his own autobiographical writings Fellini likes to describe his early days in Rome not only as a challenging time when he lived by his wits and enjoyed a feeling of adventurousness but also as a time when he experienced a certain uneasiness about his ability to remain solvent. For example, in his essay "Via Veneto: Dolce Vita," he recounts the amusing story of his unsuccessful attempt to paint an advertisement on the window of a shoe store, the same story that appears in *Moraldo in the City*, as an example

---

[4] Fellini to John C. Stubbs, Mar. 7, 1979.
[5] Solmi, *Fellini*, 68.

of how he tried to live by his wits.[6] And he comments elsewhere in the same essay, underlining his remembered uneasiness, "Rome as I knew it then was a tiny casbah of furnished rooms around the main station. . . . The fact that it was close to the station gave me a feeling of home, made me feel less far from Rimini. If things go wrong, a voice inside me kept saying, the train's there."[7]

The characters in *Moraldo in the City* provide us with new information about the people who were part of Fellini's life during this period. In a letter Fellini has stated that the character Gattone was modeled on a poet and writer of children's fables named Garrone.[8] Pinelli adds, in another letter, that Garrone did, indeed, die of acute alcoholism in the hospital on Isola Tiberina as depicted in the screenplay.[9] From the episode in "Via Veneto: Dolce Vita," we may identify the artist Lange of the screenplay as Rinaldo Geleng, now a well-known illustrator who executed the frescoes for Fellini's "Subway Sequence" in *Roma*.[10] According to Fellini, Signora Contini was based on a Signora Lenticchi,[11] and, according to Pinelli, as best he remembers, Andreina was the daughter of a custodian of the Museum of Valle Giulia.[12] (Fellini himself is discreetly silent on the subject of Andreina.)

The autobiographical content of the screenplay is well served by its episodic form. Fellini is able to treat a wide range of incidents and to create a variety of moods from the lightheartedly comic to the tenderly sad, all of which help to define the transitional period in the hero's life. Scenes with Moraldo, Lange, and Gattone in the restaurants and the Savoy Hotel are full of the good humor and camaraderie of a fine set of rogues in conspiracy. Scenes such as Moraldo's visit to Gattone in the hospital, his

---

[6] Fellini, "Via Veneto: Dolce Vita," in *Fellini on Fellini*, ed. Christian Strich (New York: Delacorte Press/Seymour Lawrence, 1976), 73-75. The essay was originally published in Italian in *L'Europeo*, 18 (8 July 1962), 49-61.

[7] *Ibid.*, 69.

[8] Fellini to Stubbs, Mar. 7, 1979.

[9] Tullio Pinelli to Stubbs, May 20, 1979.

[10] Fellini reconfirms this identification in his letter of Mar. 7, 1979.

[11] Fellini to Stubbs, Mar. 7, 1979.

[12] Pinelli to Stubbs, May 20, 1979.

refusal to return home with his father, and his good-by to
Andreina are genuinely moving, for they show Moraldo receiv-
ing or giving pain that he would much prefer to avoid, but cannot
if he is to grow. Furthermore, using a relatively open form, Fellini
is able to take time for the presentation of minor characters,
interesting in themselves, who have their moment on stage and
then disappear. "Little Hilda," Amilcare the waiter, and the
elderly office worker who blows his nose with elaborate ceremony are examples of such characters.

Despite the broad range of moods and the episodic nature of
the form, there is, nevertheless, a pleasing feel of symmetry to the
screenplay. Running through all of the episodes is the theme of
the young man from the provinces trying to find his way in the
city. In addition, the rogue characters—Gattone, Lange, and
Enrico Ricci—appear in many of the episodes from start to finish
and serve as unifying factors. Moreover, the screenplay is
divided into two symmetrical halves. (Italian movies are often
designed to accommodate an intermission in the middle, but few
are as symmetrical as this one.) In the first half major episodes
concern Moraldo's romantic entanglement with Signora Contini,
and in the second half major segments deal with his involvement
with Andreina. Both women serve as obstacles to the kind of
growth Moraldo seeks, and he has to circumvent both of them.
The episodes with the two women balance each other. The
screenplay has, then, that mixture of diversity and control that,
beginning with *I Vitelloni*, has become the mark of Fellini's best
films.

Two scenes in the screenplay are especially important
because of the use Fellini makes of them later in his career. The
first is the meeting between Moraldo and his father in Section
XXXIV. The meeting is presented mainly as a moment of temptation for Moraldo, for his father offers him the chance to return
home and give up his search for a career. In addition, though, the
scene between father and son touches on the difficulty that the
two have in being open with each other. There is a certain guard-

edness on both sides, and this wariness between father and son appears later in several of Fellini's autobiographical works. In some instances the relationship approaches overt hostility. *A Journey with Anita* treats as a central issue the hero's strained relationship with his father. In *8½* there is a friction between father and son when the father appears in a dream to complain about the size of his tomb and to check on his son's progress as a movie director. Closest to the scene in *Moraldo in the City*, however, is the situation in *La Dolce Vita* when the father of the hero Marcello comes to visit his son in Rome. Unlike Moraldo, Marcello has achieved a measure of financial success, and his father does not offer him the temptation of the family home as a refuge. Yet, as in the earlier work, we are aware of a gap between father and son that might be bridged, but is not. Marcello explains to a friend that he saw little of his father when he was young, since the father was often traveling as a salesman. In Rome Marcello tries to engage his father in conversation and to get to know him. However, Marcello's efforts to establish a closer relationship fail badly. The father suffers a mild heart attack in the apartment of a night-club dancer and, embarrassed in front of his son, leaves Rome as soon as he can. The sequence in *La Dolce Vita*, then, seems an expanded treatment of the poignant moment in *Moraldo in the City* when the father's visit to his son fails to bring the two closer.

The second scene that Fellini uses later is the last scene of the screenplay, in which a discouraged and self-doubting Moraldo walks back toward the city from the outskirts where he had fled previously. Evening lights come on. A girl smiles. A boy on a bicycle goes past, whistling a song. A pair of lovers walk along together. Gradually Moraldo's spirits rise as he regains a sense of expectancy about life. This scene is clearly a first draft version of the ending Fellini uses in *Nights of Cabiria*. In the later film Cabiria is distraught over the betrayal she has suffered at the hands of her fiancé at a lake in a resort area. As she walks away from the lake, sobbing, in the evening, a group of young people overtakes her.

They wear party hats. One boy strums a guitar, and another plays a harmonica. Two lovers ride by slowly on a Vespa. A young girl looks into the camera and says, "Good evening." And we end with a close-up of Cabiria beginning to smile. Like Moraldo, she regains a sense of interest in the attractive possibilities of life. The scene in *Nights of Cabiria* is gentler in most of its details. The people around Cabiria are more festive. But at the bottom of both scenes is the idea of life as movement or even as dance. To enter the movement or the dance is to be exhilarated. A negative version of this ending appears in *Il Bidone*, where the swindler dies near the edge of a country road, attempting to call out and reach out to a group of women and children who pass by unaware of his presence. And perhaps the famous circus finale of *8½* could be considered a highly stylized version of the ending. Here Guido attempts to direct and then joins a moving circle of people from all phases of his life. The ending of *8½*, although altered in many ways from the one in *Moraldo in the City*, seems to retain the basic idea of the protagonist's growing exhilaration as he feels himself a part of the dance or movement of life around him. The concluding scene of *Moraldo in the City*, then, seems to have provided Fellini with a piece of action, rich in metaphorical implications, which he could—and did—use later in a variety of ways.

In *Moraldo in the City* Fellini treats the transitional period between late adolescence and young adulthood in the life of his autobiographical hero. His depiction of the hero at this stage is done with humor, affection, and insight. The period has been called by psychologist Erik H. Erikson a time of "moratorium" in the formation of identity.[13] It is a stage when the late adolescent has not yet made a clear commitment to a role, or a profession, or a set of values but has broken, to some extent, from the roles and values he had as an adolescent in his home and school and is now taking the time to explore options he might pursue in the future. Moraldo is vague as to his plans for himself. In Section VIII, when Ricci asks Moraldo if he intends to be a journalist or a painter,

---

[13] Erik H. Erikson, *Identity, Youth and Crisis* (New York: Norton, 1968), 157-58.

Moraldo can only answer, "A little bit of everything." He knows only that he wants to be an autonomous adult who supports himself and is responsible for his own decisions and that he wants to try out his capabilities in a challenging arena, in this case the city, where there are real rewards to be made by success and genuine losses in failure.

This stage in life can be frightening as well as exhilarating, as Fellini knows well. Two conflicting impulses often seem to be at work.[14] One wish is to explore all the possibilities open to a late adolescent. Presumably Moraldo chose to come to the city not just because it was a challenging arena but also because it was a place where a wide range of careers, value systems, and living styles is available to him. The other wish, perhaps equally strong, is to find a secure structure for the self to replace those of the home and the school that the late adolescent has put behind him. In Moraldo's case this is the wish to replace the comfortable structures of his provincial town. The second wish, however, can be dangerous, for if the young person settles in too early, he will cut himself off from opportunities to test his potential. Moraldo is caught between these two impulses, and Fellini sets forth the conflict clearly and skillfully.

In his attempts to assert himself in the city, Moraldo fails or blunders an alarming number of times and suffers a sense of humiliation from these failures. The opening sequence, when Moraldo must absorb the rejection of his article for the newspaper, establishes the pattern. Probably even more humiliating, though, because more public, is his failure later to paint the advertisement on the window of the shoe store in proper proportion. In this instance Moraldo must absorb the hoots and criticisms of a group of on-lookers. Other moments of humiliation come when the buxom cashier rejects his plans for their Sunday afternoon outing and bids him a firm good-by in front of two chuckling pedestrians and when the grocer allows Moraldo to

---

[14] These conflicting impulses in late adolescents have been discussed succinctly and well by Gail Sheehy in *Passages: Predictable Crises of Adult Life* (New York: Bantam, 1977), 40.

give his entire sales pitch for the memorandum books only to deflate Moraldo with a single gruff phrase.

Given these rejections, in conjunction with Moraldo's dire financial straits, it is no wonder Moraldo feels the attraction of apparent havens of security when he finds them. Such refuges are provided by Signora Contini and Andreina. Both offer clearly structured relationships, with implied sets of values, that could replace the family structure in Moraldo's previous life, and, as I mentioned earlier, both present a danger to Moraldo's continued growth as an adult.

Signora Contini provides Moraldo with a firm financial base, at least for awhile, an opportunity to publish his article, and a sexual relationship with a very experienced partner. In return, however, she requires that Moraldo remain completely dependent. Certainly she requires as much or more dependency than authoritarian parents would. In fact, at her literary cocktail party she sounds very much like an overbearing mother when she instructs Moraldo, "Please try not to act bored," and promises Moraldo a trip to Taormina if he deserves the reward, or, in other words, if he is a good boy at the party. And the guests at the party understand Moraldo's position perfectly. One refers to him as "Signora Contini's boy."

Because Signora Contini's control becomes so oppressive at the party, it is relatively easy for Moraldo to break the relationship. It is much more difficult for him to free himself from Andreina's influence. Unlike Signora Contini, Andreina makes strong emotional commitments to Moraldo. The danger that Andreina poses is that the kind of middle-class life Moraldo would share with her would be severely limited, consisting of Sunday dinners followed by a nap or a radio program, a home resembling those of her parents and his, and a job in a government bureaucracy with little for Moraldo to do but wait out the day. As Moraldo realizes when he breaks his engagement, life with Andreina would offer "serene, peaceful, and sweet things." It would not, however, offer the kinds of challenges he came to the city to test himself against. This depiction of marriage as a foreclosure of personal growth is utterly consistent with Fellini's anxieties about marriage as shown in *I Vitelloni*, *8½*, *Juliet of the Spirits*, and *A Journey with Anita*.[15]

The three rogues of the screenplay, Gattone, Lange, and Ricci, are figures of encouragement for Moraldo. When the hero is most discouraged, they appear and offer ingenious plans for survival. None of the schemes works, at least in the long run. Yet these unconventional men are never without a ploy.[16] They are demonstrations to Moraldo of human resiliency. And they are embodiments of human good spirits. It is unlikely that Moraldo would have survived the challenges of the city without the emotional support of these resourceful men.

Probably the severest blow Moraldo undergoes is the death of Gattone. Of the three men, Gattone had offered the most support, and his loss is, therefore, painful for Moraldo. Furthermore, Moraldo is struck by the terrible loneliness of Gattone, who dies without any family members around him. And, most important, the death reveals to Moraldo the vulnerability of even the most resourceful and resilient of men. After the death of Gattone, then, Moraldo is especially vulnerable to his father's entreaty to return home. Moraldo is filled with despair. The nightmarish end of Lange's party serves as an outer manifestation of his inner feelings. It is a measure of Moraldo's will to remain in the city and to test himself further that he comes out of his depression at the end

---

[15] This view of marriage is certainly harsh. We could argue that marriage to Andreina might open the way for Moraldo to develop his capacity for intimacy, and Fellini is certainly aware of this need, as many of his works deal with failures in this area. But in *Moraldo in the City*, his concentration is on the negative aspect of marriage as a pulling back from experimentation with one's potential for a career and with one's possible growth as an individual. Fellini seems to imply that such experimentation must come first. In this he again follows Erikson, who argues that "true intimacy" is possible only after the "identity formation" of the young adult. Erikson, *Identity, Youth and Crisis*, 135-36.

[16] The unconventionality of the three men must be a major part of their appeal for Moraldo. They demonstrate life-styles very different from Moraldo's middle-class background and confirm his belief that there are a variety of possibilities for him to explore.

of the screenplay, refuses Ricci's aid, and reenters the movement of life on his own.

In this screenplay Moraldo achieves no breakthrough. In an American movie on a similar theme, *Next Stop, Greenwich Village* (1976), written and directed by Paul Mazursky, the young hero, an aspiring actor, obtains a role in a movie at the end and justifies his venture into Greenwich Village. There is no such clear triumph for Moraldo. All that we can conclude is that his will to test himself fully has itself been tested and has grown stronger. Through gaining this kind of internal strength, Moraldo passes out of late adolescence and into young adulthood.

Fellini wrote *A Journey with Anita* in 1957 with the help of Tullio Pinelli. The initial idea for this screenplay, which deals with a son's return with his mistress to his provincial town to see his dying father and to attend the father's funeral, came from the death of Fellini's father from a heart attack in 1956 in Fellini's native Rimini on the Adriatic. In the screenplay the town is changed to nearby Fano, and Fellini prefers not to comment on his fidelity to autobiographical details in the events surrounding his father's funeral.[17] However, some of the memories of adolescence in the provincial town that crowd back into the mind of the hero when he returns to the town are memories Fellini presented as autobiographical fact in his essay "My Rimini" (1967) and used again in his fictionalized, yet autobiographical film of adolescence, *Amarcord*.

The character of the mature, successful writer, Guido, is a version of Fellini who had achieved, by his late thirties, an international reputation based on the success of *La Strada*. The character on whom the mistress Anita was modeled, if indeed such a figure existed at all, must remain mysterious. Fellini has insisted that the character was neither modeled on nor written for Anita

---

[17] Giovanna Bentivoglio to Stubbs, June 3, 1980. In this letter Bentivoglio, Fellini's secretary, transmits a number of responses dictated by Fellini on the telephone to questions I had put to him in a letter concerning *A Journey with Anita*.

Ekberg, the Swedish actress who was to play in Fellini's next two films, *La Dolce Vita* and *The Temptations of Doctor Antonio* (1962). He has stated that he did not even know of the existence of Ekberg at the time he was writing *A Journey with Anita*.[18] The actress whom he did have in mind was Sophia Loren. And, improbably enough, the actor whom he wished for the role of Guido was Gregory Peck.[19] (To the Fellini viewer of today, it seems impossible that the part be played by anyone other than Marcello Mastroianni, so closely has this actor become identified as the screen alter ego of the mature Fellini. Yet, as was the case with Ekberg, Mastroianni did not begin to work with Fellini until *La Dolce Vita*.) Among the characters in the provincial town, we can identify Fellini's sister Maddalena as the character Gina, his plump childhood friend Titta Benzi as the lawyer Titta, and his very bright schoolmate Sega as the young doctor of Section XVI.[20]

Fellini has stated that plans for making *A Journey with Anita* collapsed when negotiations with Loren broke down, due largely to problems she was having in Italy about the legality of her marriage to producer Carlo Ponti.[21] That he did not try to continue the project with another actress may be attributable again to a hesitancy on Fellini's part to complete a work so frankly autobiographical. If Fellini was hesitant to film *Moraldo in the City*, how much more reluctant would he be with *A Journey with Anita*, which candidly depicts a strained relationship between son and father, written only a year after the father's death. The urge to make an autobiographical confession seems even stronger in *A Journey with Anita* than in *Moraldo in the City*, but concomitantly Fellini's unwillingness to film and release such an intimate film may have grown stronger also.

Although Fellini himself never made *A Journey with Anita*, a

---

[18] *Ibid.*

[19] *Ibid.*

[20] See Fellini, "My Rimini," *Fellini on Fellini*, 4-7, 13-14, 20-21, 35. Fellini's reminiscences about his childhood make clear that Benzi was the model for Titta and suggest that Sega was the young doctor.

[21] Solmi, *Fellini*, 139.

version of it, greatly changed, has been filmed. In 1978 Fellini sold the screen rights to producer Alberto Grimaldi. The producer, in turn, arranged for Mario Monicelli, Leo Benvenuti, Piero De Bernardi, Tullio Pinelli, and Paul Zimmerman to rewrite the screenplay. The movie was directed by Monicelli, and the leading roles were played by Giancarlo Giannini and Goldie Hawn. The film was released in Rome in February 1979, under the title *Viaggio con Anita* and in New York City in September 1981, under the title *Lovers and Liars*. This quite different version has been described by *Variety* reviewer Hank Werba as a "black comedy."[22] The hero of this version (Giannini) is a bank officer who takes a naïve American girl (Hawn) on a trip with him from Rome to Pisa for the funeral of his working-class father. En route they cause a car wreck, and, at the hospital where they take an injured man, they vow to start their relationship anew. On the island of Giglio, they make love. At Pisa, however, the American girl breaks off from the banker when she finds he has not been honest with her and, through her appearance at the funeral, initiates a series of scandalous revelations about the banker's family that, in essence, destroys the family. The reader will see how different Fellini's screenplay is. His main characters are both Italian. Their journey is to Fano on the Adriatic coast rather than to Pisa on the Ligurian coast. There is no automobile wreck. The Fellini journey is packed with incidents and scenes not in the movie. The family of the screenplay is middle class. And Fellini is very little concerned with unearthing family scandals. The conflicts and desires he treats run deeper than those in the rewritten film version.

Even more than was the case with *Moraldo in the City*, Fellini took materials from the screenplay of *A Journey with Anita* and reworked them for later films. For his very next movie, *La Dolce Vita*, Fellini drew on four scenes from the screenplay. One such borrowing is the scene in *La Dolce Vita*, where the party-goers visit a deserted Renaissance villa at Bassano di Sutri and Marcello, the hero, makes love to the American painter Jane in an empty room.

---

[22] Hank Werba, "Travels with Anita," *Variety*, 294 (Feb. 14, 1979), 23.

The scene is a reworking of Guido and Anita's visit to a town that has been abandoned for more than three hundred years, where they also make love. In borrowing, however, Fellini altered greatly the mood of the earlier scene. Anita breathes energy into the abandoned town in the screenplay. The party-goers of *La Dolce Vita*, on the other hand, seem to succumb to the sense of ruin and exhaustion in the old villa. It is as if Fellini decided to use the setting of the abandoned site in *La Dolce Vita* for a purpose exactly opposite to the one he intended originally in *A Journey with Anita*. Another borrowing is the scene in the nightclub in the Baths of Caracalla of *La Dolce Vita*, where the Hollywood star Sylvia abandons Marcello as a dance partner and breaks into an exhibitionistic and energetic dance with a satyrlike partner. The dance seems to be another version of the one Anita performs at the farmhouse in *A Journey with Anita*. In both instances, it is the pagan, sexual explosiveness of the women that Fellini wants to capture. Still another borrowing comes from the car scene in *A Journey with Anita*, where Guido attacks Anita verbally for her behavior with the workers, forces her from the car, and then returns to her later to find her seated confidently on a wall, filing her nails. In *La Dolce Vita* the scene becomes an argument between Marcello and his mistress Emma over her possessive, maternal love. Fellini supplies a bit more physical comedy here. First, Emma gets out angrily from the car on her own volition, and Marcello must urge her to climb back in. Then, as the argument continues, he gets out of the car, tugs her from it, and, resuming his place, drives off without her. When he returns later, he finds her pacing the side of the road, holding a bunch of flowers she has gathered. She is almost as triumphant, if not as serene, as Anita. A final borrowing is Fellini's ending of *La Dolce Vita*. The film concludes with close-ups of the face of Paola, the young girl from Umbria, as she smiles sadly and waves good-by to Marcello when he rejoins his friends from Rome. In the conclusion of *A Journey with Anita* Guido drives off from the cemetery, leaving behind the waving Anita, who seems "so gentle and loving that his sadness is not without a shimmer of joy." Both women represent a simple and attractive life of the past that the heroes, for better or worse, have moved beyond.

For *8½* Fellini does not borrow scenes from *A Journey with Anita*, but he does go over two subjects first presented in the screenplay. The dream scene in *8½*, already discussed, in which Guido's father complains about the size of his tomb, seems a continuation of the salespitch Eugenio gives Guido in Section XIX of the screenplay to build an elaborate tomb with altar and bench. It is apparent from the description of the tomb in the last scene of the screenplay that Guido resisted Eugenio's high-pressured sales attempt, but it is also apparent from the dream in *8½* that the autobiographical hero feels a certain amount of guilt over settling for the smaller tomb. A second subject is the somewhat uncomfortable Oedipal situation between son and mother that appears in both works. In the screenplay Guido spends a night in his father's place in the parents' double bed with his mother, and in *8½*, in his dream about his parents, Guido ushers his father back into his tomb and then receives a passionate kiss from his mother, who eventually changes into the character of his wife. (A somewhat comic version of the Oedipal situation occurs also in *Roma*, where a sunburnt son curls up in bed with his enormous mother before the eyes of the amazed young protagonist on his first day in Rome.) Interesting in Fellini's transfer of the material from the screenplay to *8½* is that he puts the Oedipal tensions into a dream in *8½*. It may be that Fellini is more comfortable with such material on the more abstract level of dream than he is on the level of straightforward, realistic representation.

Two events surrounding the death of Guido's father in the screenplay may have provided material for Fellini's presentation of the death of the mother of Titta, the young protagonist in *Amarcord*. The mysteriously prompt arrival of relatives and friends in the screenplay seems repeated in the equally prompt arrival of friends and relatives at Titta's house the morning after the mother's death during the night. In the later version it is this arrival that informs Titta of his mother's death. The funeral in Sections XXVIII and XXIX of the screenplay also seems to provide elements that appear in the services for Titta's mother in *Amarcord*. Whereas the service in church in the screenplay is marred by the comings and goings of people and the screeching of benches, the more solemn funeral service in *Amarcord* is spoiled by the fainting of Titta's uncle. The funeral corteges in both works move through the town in weather that is inappropriately bright. In fact, in *Amarcord*, we learn that the day is the first of spring, when puff-ball clusters of seeds blow through the air. In both works, then, there is a sense of one life ending and other lives continuing.

Finally, there are three episodes in the screenplay that Fellini retells later as autobiographical material in the essay "My Rimini" and then employs in fictionalized form in *Amarcord*. One involves the restaurant by the sea in the screenplay, which Guido as an adolescent felt was a glittering, magic spot where luxury, wealth, and sophistication were on display. In "My Rimini" the place is identified not as a restaurant but as the terrace of the Grand Hotel. Fellini writes, "In the evening, the Grand Hotel became Istanbul, Bagdad, Hollywood. On its terraces, curtained by thick rows of plants, the Ziegfeld Follies might have been taking place. We caught glimpses of barebacked women who looked marvelous to us, clasped in the arms of men in white dinner-jackets."[23] In *Amarcord* Fellini gives us a sequence on the terrace of the Grand Hotel in which Titta and his adolescent friends watch the older males in white dinner jackets romance the gowned female tourists. The restaurant of *A Journey with Anita*, however, seems disappointingly ordinary to Guido when he returns to it as an adult. Perhaps this double view of the screenplay carries over also into *Amarcord*, for while we begin with the point of view of the bedazzled adolescents on the outside, we move in closer to look at the lovers in action and to overhear the cliché qualities of their lines. The other two events Fellini uses later involve Gradisca, the

---

[23] Fellini, "My Rimini," *Fellini on Fellini*, 20.

well-endowed vamp of the provincial town. One is the story of how she got her name, which means "Please help yourself," in the course of seducing a visiting official, and the other is the story of how the hero as an adolescent moved closer to her in a movie theater, attempted a sexual overture, and was casually dismissed. Both stories are repeated in similar detail in "My Rimini" and filmed with little change in *Amarcord*. The two stories go well together. The one sets up Gradisca as a legendary figure whose seductiveness is such that she can secure rewards for her town with it, and the second shows the adolescent hero's yearning for this legendary woman, who is an ultimate to him in sexual experience and desirability. After her presentation in *Amarcord*, Gradisca has certainly become one of Fellini's most memorable characters. The two brief anecdotes concerning her in *A Journey with Anita* mark his first attempt to use this figure from his adolescent past as a character in one of his works.

As is the case with *Moraldo in the City* and the films after *I Vitelloni*, the form of *A Journey with Anita* is open. The journey to Fano provides a unifying element, but each of the discrete sequences and scenes makes its own impact. The episodes seem designed especially to evoke mood or establish aspects of character, rather than to tell formal stories-within-the-story with beginnings, middles, and ends. Particularly effective is the sequence involving the church fresco and the celebration of the Night of San Giovanni in Sections VIII-IX. The sequence has that mixture of comedy, strong feeling, and unusual atmosphere that appears often in Fellini's best episodes. We learn how Guido and his mistress differ in their responses to the church and the Madonna of Piero della Francesca, and we see in full measure Anita's sensuality and Guido's reaction to it. But best of all, the custodian's family and their folk traditions are interesting in themselves, and even—the words are not too much—mysterious and profound. (It seems odd that having later used so many of the other scenes from the screenplay Fellini never found place for this set piece on folk culture.) Wonderfully lyrical in *A Journey with Anita* are the vignettes of the big country breakfast in Section VI, Guido's walk on the main street of Fano in the dazzling sunshine in Section XV, the coming of the dawn as Guido sees it from the hotel balcony in Section XVIII with the women on bicycles bringing their produce to market, and his drive in the evening along the seafront in Section XXIV, when the orchestras play for the tourists and fireworks explode overhead. Touching and sad is the brief scene in Section XIX, where Titta's father slips behind some plants in his garden to avoid meeting Guido and having to speak of the death of Guido's father. This scene is one of several delicately drawn sketches of reactions to the death of Guido's father. In addition to such lyric or affecting scenes the work is filled with comic characters and comic moments that help fill out our picture of the provincial world and also save it from being saccharine. These characters include the pompous doctor, the shy but mildly flirtatious mother superior, and Eugenio, the overly ambitious sculptor; the moments include the scene between Titta and the farmer in the law office, the story of the father whacking Guido and Titta with the umbrella, and the two anecdotes about Gradisca that were discussed earlier. The open form, then, allows Fellini to create here, as he does elsewhere when he is successful, a work that is profuse in mood and rich in details of human behavior.

Fellini's presentation of the city in *A Journey with Anita* differs markedly from the depiction of the city in *Moraldo in the City*. Here the city is no longer a place of challenge, for Fellini's hero in *A Journey with Anita* has met all of its tests. The city now seems a sophisticated adult world lacking both the qualities of spontaneity and direct, unmasked emotional responses that he knew as a child and adolescent in his provincial town and also the kind of security and sense of well-being he felt there. At the opening of the screenplay, Fellini shows us Guido's sense of disengagement from his city life. We witness the artificiality of the literary cocktail party, the formality and distance between Guido and his upper-middle-class wife, and even the uncomfortable newness of his home. The depiction of the city in this screenplay is different from

the one in *Moraldo in the City* because the hero is different. Guido
has achieved the kind of success in his career that Moraldo longs
for so desperately, and Guido wishes to recapture now some of
the elements of his past that he apparently put aside during his
rise to success. Guido, in short, has a midlife crisis. He wants to
regain lost capacities before it is too late.

The theme of the return to the provincial home is one of the
dominant subjects in modern Italian literature. Industrialization
in Italy has caused major population shifts, and with these shifts
there have come longings on the part of many to recapture what
was lost in the move from the native home. The two most important
writers of modern Italian fiction, Cesare Pavese and Elio Vittorini,
for example, have treated the theme of the return to the provincial
home. In *The Moon and the Bonfires* (1953), Pavese depicts his
hero's return to an area of Piedmont after he has made his fortune
in the United States. The hero wishes to reestablish a rapport with
the land and the people of the region that he never found in the
United States. He wishes to discover stability. In all this he fails,
for his region and his friends have changed, and the hero is,
sadly, as alien in his native land as he was in America. In *Conversation in Sicily* (1939), however, Vittorini shows a hero who
returns, almost by chance, to Sicily from his life in northern Italy
and regenerates his sexual, political, and moral energies as he follows his mother on her rounds as a practical nurse and becomes
involved in the plottings of a Resistance group. Fellini's *A Journey
with Anita* seems to draw on both Vittorini's positive depiction
and Pavese's negative version of the return.

The provincial town is important to Guido for its reassuring
stability and the deeply felt and sincerely expressed emotions of
its citizens. He feels at peace in the provincial town. Fano has its
daily rituals. And death, that ultimately disruptive force, is itself
ritualized elaborately by the townspeople. The nuns must be
invited to pray and sing at the vigil. The mourners must be fed.
The body must be transferred to the church for a final mass. The
funeral cortege has its established pattern. A world with so much

form would doubtless seem constraining to Moraldo, but to the older Guido it offers a certain comfort. The discovery of "the continuing existence of an ancient world," whose forms are repeated over and over, gives him a sense of being part of a continuity greater than any individual life can have.

More important, perhaps, Guido discovers a genuineness of emotion in the feelings of townspeople, friends, and relatives concerning the truly important event of a human death. Fellini writes, "Everywhere [Guido] went, he encountered old friends and acquaintances. All of them were genuinely saddened by his father's death. They said over and over like a refrain, 'He was so cheerful he made everyone else feel good.'" The people of the provincial town show their feelings directly. An old friend of the father, for example, enters the house shortly after the father dies and "goes directly to kneel by the bed without having the strength to say a word." Furthermore, Guido encounters and feels the strength of familial emotional ties. (The continuing importance of the family is another element in the town's stability.) A striking example of this is the scene in which Guido's mother in her grief wanders through the house after the body has been taken to the church, enters the room where the body lay, and holds a conversation with her husband's spirit. By coming into contact with such strongly felt emotions, Guido himself regains a capacity to feel.

However, Guido as an adult has become an intellectual. His response to the Madonna of Piero della Francesca, mentioned earlier, is refined and aesthetic, not simple and religious, as Anita's is. Guido carries with him sophisticated, cultural frames of reference, and he exhibits what is perhaps a curse to Fellini, the intellectual's tendency to be reflective and analytical. While not without a certain spontaneity, Guido does have the tendency to play back events in his mind and search through them for all their possible implications. This he does with Anita's actions at the farmhouse when he is in the car the next morning, with the events of the day his father died when he is in Anita's hotel room, and with his relationship with his father when he recounts it to Anita at the restaurant on the wharf. Guido is, in other words, a bit too sophisticated or too intellectual for the simple provincial world to which he returns, and he is, therefore, cut off from it at the same time that he admires it and draws from it a renewed capacity to feel.

If it seems likely that Fellini drew on Italian literary tradition, as I think is the case, it is perhaps even more likely that he drew on the archetype of the journey of the hero in myth and folklore to a confrontation with a parent figure. In *The Hero with a Thousand Faces*, anthropologist Joseph Campbell outlines a pattern that many myths and folktales retell. A hero receives a mysterious call. He leaves his region of safety and passes into a mysterious land where he undergoes a series of tests. He is often aided by a supernatural being or a mentor. The adventures help prepare him for a supreme ordeal that very often involves confrontation with a parent figure. The hero gains or loses his reward and returns to his starting point.[24] Many elements of this archetypal pattern appear in Fellini's screenplay, whether by conscious design or because Fellini tapped the same basic wishes and fears of the mythmakers and the tellers of folktales. These elements give Fellini's work a resonance it would not otherwise have.

The call in Fellini's screenplay is the message he receives on the telephone. It is mysterious in that Guido cannot make it out clearly. Furthermore, its garbled nature gives Guido the option of rejecting the invitation to make the trip, as is often the case in the archetype where sometimes the hero does reject the call and suffers dire consequences.

The mentor figure is Anita. She is one of the earliest of the large, fleshy women who have become trademarks in Fellini's

---

[24]Joseph Campbell, *The Hero with a Thousand Faces* (Princeton: Princeton University Press, 1968). For purposes of simplification, I have suppressed some elements of Campbell's outline that do not have counterparts in *A Journey with Anita*. The suppression, however, does not weaken my argument, for very few myths contain *all* of the elements Campbell names. The important point is that a significant number of the elements are present in *A Journey with Anita*.

films and who are usually associated with sexual energy, strong emotions, and even a certain amount of fearsome power.[25] In her function as a mentor, or aiding goddess figure, Anita is strikingly similar to Saraghina in *8½* and Suzy in *Juliet of the Spirits*. Anita's role is to school Guido in the art of feeling. This she does with her appetite for food, with her spontaneous reactions to the abandoned town and to the rites of the Night of San Giovanni, and with the jealousy she arouses in Guido by her behavior among the workers at the blast site. In brief she prepares Guido for his reentry into the world of strongly felt emotions of his past.

The major ordeal is the funeral of Guido's father. Campbell argues that the supreme test in myth and folklore often involves the resolution of the Oedipal conflict either by a sacred marriage with a goddess-mother or by atonement with a god-father figure. In *A Journey with Anita*, Guido literally replaces his father in his mother's bed for one night. The result is not, however, an overthrow of the father, but rather a reconciliation with the father.

According to Campbell's Freudian reading of the archetype, the father appears as an enemy to his son because he is the figure who first challenged the son's blissful one-to-one relationship with the mother and because he is superior to his son in mastery of experience in the adult world. In *A Journey with Anita*, however, Fellini offers reasons for friction between father and son that are more specific. First, there is the lack of understanding between the father who wanted a conventional life for his son and the son who wanted to pursue a more daring, intellectual course. Second, there is the resentment of the son for the father based on the son's awareness of the pain the father's infidelities have given to the mother. These two causes fuel an antagonism in Guido. We see it in Guido's comic description of the long periods of time his father devoted to digesting his meals and in Guido's hesitancy to

---

[25] Fellini has always been interested in the symbolic roles that have been assigned to women by the male imagination. (This interest has, of course, earned him the distrust of feminist critics who wish to have women presented as women, not just as male fantasy figures.) He has remarked, "Man has always been accustomed to

return to his father's bedside until Guido decides to combine filial duty with a pleasurable escape with Anita. Yet when Guido learns of his father's apparent recovery, Guido is pleased, and, when he reaches his father, Guido seems to hope for more in the way of reconciliation than his father's somewhat ambiguous question, "Guido, now why did you go to all the trouble of coming?"

Reconciliation with the father comes after the father's death. Looking at his father's body on the bed, Guido "has the strange sensation that he sees himself in the body of his father. . . . Every part of that immobile body seems rooted in Guido. The hands are different, and the lines of the face, the ears and the forehead, all different. Yet the differences seem only variations of a certain theme or model." Then the next night Guido takes his father's place in the matrimonial bed. And twice later Guido equates affairs his father had with the woman in the florist shop and the woman Guido sees crying at the funeral procession with Guido's own affair with Anita. Certainly Guido comes to understand his father better. The meeting with Brother Elijah, the father's friend, helps. But more important is that Guido discovers and acknowledges a continuity between the man his father was and the man Guido is. Here he finds yet another source of comfort, and again he discovers he is part of a continuum greater than the life of a single person.

A Journey with Anita, written a year after the death of Fellini's father, gives us perhaps the most extended treatment in the Fellini canon of the Oedipal conflict between father and son. We have already noted that Fellini treats friction or lack of closeness between the father and the son in *Moraldo in the City*, *La Dolce Vita*, and *8½*. In none of these is there a reconciliation. The Oedipal

look at woman as a mystery onto which he projects his fantasies. She is mother, wife or whore, or Dante's Beatrice or the muse. Man through the ages has continued to cover woman's face with masks that to his subconscious, probably, represented the unknown part of himself." Quoted in Jay Cocks, "Fellini Remembers," *Time*, 104 (Oct. 7, 1974), 11.

conflict, transferred to mother and daughter, does have a resolution of sorts in *Juliet of the Spirits*, but it comes through the painful
self-assertion of Juliet against her mother in a dream sequence.
Amarcord, however, like *A Journey with Anita*, offers a positive
resolution to the conflict. In this film the father and son who have
been antagonists throughout most of the action achieve a kind of
reconciliation through their shared grief over the death of the
mother. It is interesting that the two gentle reconciliations, those
of *A Journey with Anita* and *Amarcord*, come in films about the provincial town. Fellini seems to see as one of the finest possibilities
of the provincial town in his symbolic polarity between city and
town the chance that reconciliation between father and son can
occur there.

Moraldo in the City* and *A Journey with Anita* are interesting in
their own right. *Moraldo in the City* is a fine, humorous account of
a young man's entry into the city in search of adulthood, and *A
Journey with Anita* is a moving account of a mature man's return to
his provincial town in quest of elements of his past he can value
and draw nourishment from. But the screenplays are also important in fleshing out more fully our view of Fellini's *oeuvre*. They
provide early draft versions of scenes, situations, and characters
that Fellini drew on in later works. To examine these early draft
versions is to examine early stages in the creative process of the
filmmaker. These screenplays also give further instances of
Fellini's experimentation with open form in the 1950s, when he
was beginning to tell stories, establish characters, and create
moods in an episodic manner. For those interested in the life of
the artist behind the work, these two screenplays offer details,
people, and leads that can be enjoyed in themselves and then
investigated further. Most important, perhaps, *Moraldo in the City*
and *A Journey with Anita* provide us with new and quite exciting
pieces in Fellini's continuing portrayal of an autobiographical
hero whom Fellini likes to study at transitional moments. This
hero cuts across many works from *I Vitelloni* to *Amarcord*. He may

not be more interesting in himself than are the individual works that contain him (as is the case, for example, with Sherlock Holmes), but he is at least as interesting as the best of the individual works. The hero is, in a sense, a work that viewers create in their own minds from the Fellini films about the hero. Now, with the publication of *Moraldo in the City* and *A Journey with Anita*, the hero is a little more fully defined and richly drawn, even if we must find the new pieces of him in screenplays and not, sadly enough, in films.

Moraldo in the City

By Federico Fellini
With Ennio Flaiano and Tullio Pinelli

PART ONE

I

"Is Signor Blasi here?"

The male receptionist of the editorial office looks up at a modestly dressed young man in front of him. The receptionist rubs his forehead, passes a hand over his face, and yawns. He has no inclination to answer. Finally he decides to speak: "Do you have an appointment?"

"Yes, at 5:00."

"What's your name?"

"Rubini. Moraldo Rubini. Signor Blasi knows me."

The receptionist looks at the young man again, yawns with great gusto, and at last gives the predictable answer: "No one is here."

Should he leave? Moraldo Rubini hesitates before going back into the hot streets of that August afternoon.

Three months ago he left his hometown and his gang of friends to come to Rome in search of decent work and above all in search of himself. He feels the need for a purpose in life different from that of others his age. But what purpose? He is bewildered. He had been getting by on the little bit of money that he had brought with him and on a money order sent to him by his mother. Everywhere he turned he received only vague promises, and now, in the middle of summer, his thoughts return nostalgically to his hometown, where certainly the swimming season has begun and where his friends are surely enjoying themselves, sheltered from all economic worries.

This translation is based on the Italian version printed in *Cinema* (nuova serie), 12 (1954), 459-62, 593-94, 657-58, 686, 718, 743-44.

Should he leave? Should he give up? The only hope that he has is the promise given to him by Blasi, a journalist whom he met in a *trattoria*. Blasi promised to publish one of his articles and launch him in journalism. He told Moraldo to stop by the editorial office at 5:00 P.M., but now no Blasi.

"Can I wait?"

The reception shows him a door. "Wait in there for a little while."

In the waiting room there is a man writing at a table. He hardly raises his head at Moraldo's entry, but he acknowledges Moraldo's greeting with a smile that is almost childish or, at any rate, unusual. He is middle-aged, with a ruddy complexion. He has the marked features of a cheerful pleasure-seeker, and his smile expresses a boyish joyfulness.

After a moment the man turns to Moraldo: "By any chance, do you have a cigarette?" He has a northern accent, and his request is made with the ease of one who habitually asks favors of strangers. He takes the cigarette that Moraldo offers to him, waits for a light from Moraldo, and then thanks him.

"Gian Antonio Gattone," he says at last, stretching out his hand.

"Moraldo Rubini. Pleased to meet you."

Gattone resumes writing, as if forgetting his new acquaintance. Then suddenly he asks: "Do you write?"

"Well, I'm beginning," Moraldo answers modestly.

"Listen to this then," says Gattone. He snatches up a sheet of paper and reads: "The small carriage of Parmesan cheese with four wonderful wheels of provolone had become stuck in the lane of butter. In vain the two fiery steeds of ricotta tried to draw the carriage forth from its critical situation. I don't need to tell you at this point, my dear little friends, how great was the fear of the coachman of mascarpone, who was cracking his whip made of strings of mozzarella!"

Smiling, Gattone looks at Moraldo. "How does that seem to you as a beginning?"

"It's good," says Moraldo, also smiling.

"It's a fable," says Gattone. "I am now contributing to the children's page in the newspaper. But would you believe that while writing I have become hungry?"

"I believe it," Moraldo answers. And then he asks immediately, "Excuse me, you said you were Gian Antonio Gattone?"

"Yes."

"You are the author of 'Won't You Travel with Me?'"

Gattone sits back, a little amazed. "But that was ten years ago!" he says at last, flattered to have discovered a reader with such a good memory.

"I used to read your column always. It was marvelous," Moraldo says enthusiastically. "It used to give me a wild urge to travel. I wanted to be an explorer. Then, after that. . . ." And he makes a gesture as if to say: "I have never read anything else of yours. What happened?"

"Life. This filthy, lovely, awful life!" exclaims Gattone. "What would you expect, my good friend? I had to try all the professions. But now I intend to take up writing again." And while Moraldo nods his head in approval, Gattone continues, "Oh, yes, I am taking up writing again. I still have so many things to tell, a suitcase full of notes. The fables allow me to keep going. I do not sign them. That is, I sign them GAT."

"Hello poet," a voice interrupts ironically from behind them. They turn. In the door is a small, thin, dressed-up young man who smiles as if he had discovered a very amusing scene that he will recount to friends outside in the editorial office. It is Blasi.

"I am working for you, my friend," exclaims Gattone, waving his sheets of paper. He is truly happy to see Blasi. He has no suspicion of the ironic intentions in Blasi's eyes because Gattone is a candid soul and measures other people in terms of his own good will.

"Good. Work on. Stay with it," continues Blasi, still ironically. At last Blasi turns to Moraldo, this time more serious, even a bit worried. "You came about that material?"

Standing up, Moraldo waits to hear the sentence that he fears will not be favorable because Blasi seems annoyed.

"There's a difficulty," Blasi says.

Moraldo has a wan smile on his face. He is incapable of saying a word. He had never really believed his piece would be accepted, but now he is certain that it will be rejected.

"The editor says that it won't do. I'm sorry." Already Blasi is rummaging in his pockets. He pulls out a crumpled manuscript that he returns to Moraldo, pleased to have rid himself of the problem so hastily.

"You can try again," he says consolingly, getting another wan smile from Moraldo, who does not want to seem a nuisance and does not protest. Then, drawing Blasi out of trouble, Gattone cries, "I need to see the managing director. I have absolute, peremptory, urgent need."

"The managing director? Forget it, my good friend," declares Blasi. After addressing other general words of encouragement to Moraldo, Blasi uses the pretext of urgent work as an excuse for sneaking away. "Come see me again sometime. I am always here at five."

Meanwhile, Gattone has finished writing. He folds his papers and starts to the door. Noticing that Moraldo is about to go outside, too, he calls to him, "Wait a second. I'll go with you."

II

The *trattoria* that Moraldo and Gattone have entered for supper is one of those restaurants in the neighborhood of the train station, with meals at a fixed price, empty tables, the usual refrigerator against a wall, and a single, elderly waiter with flat feet, who is shabby and melancholy.

"You eat very well here," exclaims Gattone as he enters, in order to ingratiate himself with the owner, the typically beefy man behind the cash register. They sit at the best table, study the menu at length, place their order, call back the waiter, cancel the order previously given, and look at another more elaborate menu. "And wine, wine, wine," repeats Gattone happily, rubbing his hands together. The prospect of an enjoyable evening with a new friend who is an admirer enlivens him and makes him loquacious. Soon he is in the middle of an account of his adventures in Mexico with a very beautiful woman. Then he stops.

From the rest room comes a new person, drying his hands. When he sees Gattone, he throws his arms up in enthusiasm. Introductions are made. The new friend is the painter Lange, a young man about thirty. He is tall and has a wolfish face with an enormous smile that flashes continually.

"You in this neighborhood, too?"

"Yes."

"How is Lisa?"

"She went off with a big industrialist, but she'll be back."

They laugh together, mentioning mutual acquaintances and slapping each other on the back. The waiter, meanwhile, arrives carrying a bottle of wine. Immediately Gattone becomes serious and pours glasses of wine for the first toast. "To a long life," he says, raising his glass.

From behind the cash register, the owner, darkly worried, watches the three of them as they drink. Their type of cheerfulness is the kind that does not bode well for him.

III

The dinner has lasted a long time. It was an abundant meal. The table is covered with bottles and half-bottles. The waiter Amilcare is in the process of folding up the tablecloths of the other tables. The *trattoria* is deserted except for our three friends and a couple of latecomers who are finishing up their meal hastily.

Our friends are silent. They are looking intently at a drawing that Lange is completing. The drawing shows Gattone, Moraldo, and Lange bowing to the owner and saying, "Put it on the tab until tomorrow night." They have discovered, in fact, that all three of them together do not have enough money to pay the bill. They have decided against paying any of it at all and have agreed to use the ploy of the drawing.

"You think that he will go for this?" asks Gattone.

"Why wouldn't he?" says Lange. "The drawing alone is worth more than what we ate."

Moraldo agrees, although he shares fully the doubts of Gattone. He is swept along.

Lange has now finished the drawing, and he is the first to laugh at the ploy, which seems excellent to him. He folds the drawing twice and calls the waiter. "Would you give this to the manager?" he asks.

The waiter takes the sheet of paper. He would like to say something, but his expression is eloquent enough. He knows the boss.

The owner is in the back of the room. He has been following the suspicious maneuvers, and without smiling he watches the waiter's approach. He takes the sheet of paper and, with hardly a glance at it, stuffs it into his pocket.

"Let's order a little more wine," proposes Gattone. Lange finds the proposal amusingly extravagant, and he laughs until he is on the verge of tears.

Now for our three friends it's a matter of awaiting the owner's reaction. He, however, seems not to want to pay attention to their prank. Passing the table of our three friends without looking at them, he makes up the bill for the couple of latecomers. After the couple leaves, the manager advances to the table. "Well, what are we going to do here?" he says sullenly, a little threateningly.

The three look at him without answering. How could it be? He is not enjoying their prank. Is this possible?

"What are we going to do here?" repeats the manager slowly. The waiter watches the scene, leaning on the cash register. From the kitchen the cook and his female helper poke their heads out.

"Did you see our drawing?" Lange asks finally.

"Never mind the drawing. What are we going to do here?" repeats the manager.

As a man of importance, Gattone feels offended. "Well, excuse me," he says, "but since we asked you for a favor, you could at least have the decency to answer us."

The manager squints at Gattone and at Moraldo. The latter would like to crawl under the table.

"If you don't have money, why do you eat?" he says at last with all the contempt a restaurant owner can muster.

"For your information, we have money, plenty of money. But it would be kind of you to wait until tomorrow night for it, as we asked in the drawing," says Gattone. And he adds, "We will come here often to eat, you know."

"No, I don't want you here," says the manager darkly and calmly. He leans over the table on his hands, looks steadily at the three of them, and repeats slowly, "I do not want you in here."

The manager moves back a step. He is beginning to lose his patience, but he restrains himself. "Don't make jokes with me. Understand? To me your jokes aren't funny!"

The three are silent and immobile. They avoid looking at the manager.

"Tomorrow evening – " says Lange.

"No, never. Get out and don't come back any more. Out! Outside, all of you," finishes the manager, throwing the drawing on the table. Then he storms off into the kitchen, furious.

The waiter Amilcare, who feared worse, breathes a sigh of relief.

Our three friends get up. Lange picks up the drawing. The three move toward the door, in silence, without looking at each other.

"Good evening," Gattone calls back politely as he leaves the restaurant. He acts as though nothing had happened. He has been through worse moments than this in his life.

"Good evening," Amilcare responds softly.

IV

Moraldo, Gattone, and Lange walk through one of the streets in the neighborhood of the station. Gattone has recovered his confidence completely, and he minimizes the incident. He is surprised, however, that the other two have no money.

"I have maybe three hundred lire," says Lange. "I had gone in for an order of spaghetti, and then what happened happened."

"And you, Moraldo, how much do you have?"

Moraldo pulls from his pockets everything he has, two hundred lire.

"There's nothing to worry about. Tomorrow I am going to collect on my stories for this month. We'll eat better tomorrow than we did this evening. It has all been a misunderstanding. I thought that you, Moraldo, had money."

"And I thought that you had invited me," says Moraldo.

"Yes, I invited you," Gattone sets it straight, "but I had no way of knowing you were out of money."

The three laugh. Now that the painful scene in the restaurant is only a memory, they laugh about it until they come to tears.

"To finish the evening, let's phone some girls. Let's phone the two sisters," suggests Gattone.

Lange finds the proposal unreasonable and makes the excuse that it is late.

"What do you mean late?" exclaims Gattone hurt and astonished. "It's barely midnight."

Here one of the problems with Gattone's life-style is revealed. For him, the evening cannot "get late." The people at his hotel have confiscated his suitcase and put him out until he pays his bill.

"I can't pay it until tomorrow. So tonight, I'll make my way around the city. It's summer. I'll look at the stars. And Moraldo will come with me."

V

At 2:00 A.M. Gattone and Moraldo stop in front of a door in the Viale delle Milizia.

"Only for tonight," insists Gattone. "Is it a problem for you?"

"The difficulty is that I don't have a key for the front door," says Moraldo.

"No key? How come?"

"I owe a month's rent, and the concierge has used this as an excuse to take back my door key. So in the evening I have to wait until someone else comes back, and then I can go in with that person."

"And what if no one comes back?" asks Gattone, alarmed.

"Someone always comes back. But if nobody does, I have to call the concierge." Moraldo points to a window on the second floor.

Some time passes. The street is deserted.

"This is getting annoying," Gattone says.

"I'll call," says Moraldo with a sigh. He goes underneath the window and calls timidly, "Signora." No one answers.

"Signora," Moraldo calls more energetically.

"Nobody heard you. You have to shout," urges Gattone.

Moraldo continues to call. At first he is more forceful, but then afraid of waking the other tenants, softer, dropping his last syllables and varying his voice. Finally a window opens, but it is a window on the mezzanine. A heavy-set man leans out in his undershirt, sleepy and sullen. "Every night it is something," he mutters, irritated.

"I forgot my key," explains Moraldo in a soft voice.

"Yes, you forget it every night," states the man. Then he turns back toward the interior of the room and talks to a person who evidently has remained in bed, "He says he forgot his key."

Turning back to Moraldo, the heavy-set man says, "The concierge doesn't let you have a key, does she?"

"I forgot that," says Moraldo.

The man disappears from the window. In a few minutes the door opens. The man walks out in his slippers and socks. "Come in," he says, "otherwise you'll be out there all night."

Moraldo and Gattone enter quickly, thanking the man. Gattone doesn't miss the chance to act the part of a man of the world. "You are a gentleman," he says, and he introduces himself.

The heavy-set man follows them to the stairs, yawning. "Make her give you a key," he advises. By now he has become good-natured and has taken a liking to them.

VI

"What a very nice room," says Gattone, entranced. Moraldo motions to him to lower his voice.

Gattone sits on the sofa. "I'll sleep here. I'm used to it. I don't want to inconvenience you," he tells Moraldo. With a sigh of relief, Gattone takes off his shoes. Then he looks over Moraldo's books, takes one of them, and observes that there is no lamp near the sofa.

"I like to read before I go to sleep," he says.

"Take my lamp, there on the night table," offers Moraldo.

While Gattone is settling down for the night, the concierge of the building enters in her night clothes. She is a woman approximately forty-five years old, and she looks very much like a landlady. Her surprise at finding the room occupied by two tenants is surpassed only by her surprise at the enthusiastic reception Gattone gives her. One would think he was the guest of a nineteenth-century chatelaine. He offers her an endless series of thanks and bows.

"Come out with me for a minute," says the concierge to Moraldo finally. He follows her into the corridor and then into the kitchen, where the concierge starts to complain vigorously about the state of affairs.

"It's only for tonight," Moraldo says imploringly.

"Not forever? That would be all I need!" replies the concierge.

Moraldo explains that these things can happen. Signor Gattone is a friend, a famous writer, unexpectedly forced to seek hospitality. As Moraldo talks, the concierge calms down.

"Who let you in?"

"A man from the mezzanine."

The concierge becomes quiet. She looks at Moraldo and smiles. "You're quite a young man, you are," she says.

Moraldo feels the approach of a moment of tenderness that he fears more than terrible moments from the concierge.

"Have you eaten tonight?"

"Yes, thanks."

"I'm listening. What did you eat?"

"Well, a lot of stuff. I was invited."

"Wouldn't you like me to fix you two eggs? You're young. You have to eat."

"I have already eaten, I told you."

The concierge smiles, tidies her hair, and pulls tight her robe coquettishly. "What a deceiver! You do it so I can't have my way." She smiles again and then stretches her hand out to caress Moraldo's head.

"When I heard you come back," she says, "I thought you were with a woman."

"And if there had been a woman?"

The concierge shakes her fist and smiles invitingly. Then she steers the conversation skillfully to Moraldo's back rent, hinting at the possibility that the two of them might be able to reach some understanding about the matter. Moraldo protests that he will pay in a few days. His strategy is to pretend not to understand her innuendos. He thanks the concierge and wishes her a good night.

When Moraldo reenters his room, he finds Gattone snoring, with the book open on his chest and the lamp lit. Moraldo looks at him, extinguishes the light, and then goes to the window to meditate on his difficult situation.

VII

It is a warm morning in August. The streets going out from the Piazza Risorgimento are almost deserted. The Romans are all at the seashore. In one of these streets walks Moraldo looking for an address. He stops in front of a doorway. "Excuse me. The magazine *Life and Letters*?"

"Number four, Signora Contini," answers the doorman.

Moraldo goes up the stairs. A little later, a pretty maid shows him into a reception room that also serves as a storage area for back copies of the magazine *Life and Letters*. Stacks of them rise toward the ceiling.

"Signora Contini?"

"Who should I say wants to see her?"

"Here, I have a letter." Moraldo takes out a letter from his pocket. Then in order to establish with the maid his lengthy experience in matters of the literary world, he nods at the bundles cluttering the room and asks, "Are all the issues here?"

"What do you mean, all the issues?" answers the maid. "There has been only one issue published."

"Only one?"

"That's right. She is working on the second one now."

The maid disappears into the interior of the suite and then returns after a few minutes. "Please, come with me." She leads Moraldo through the wide corridor filled with printed material and Savonarola chairs. They come to a study with Renaissance-style furniture, some paintings, and some bookcases. "One moment, please."

Behind a table, absorbed in her work, sits Signora Contini. She is a beautiful woman in her mid-thirties, with a proud nose and the eyes of a person accustomed to giving orders and to having them carried out. For awhile, she continues her work without looking at Moraldo, in her usual manner for impressing new acquaintances. She knows that Moraldo is still standing and is looking at her.

"Sit down," she says dryly.

Ill at ease, Moraldo takes a seat. Signora Contini takes up his letter and rereads it. "You are a close friend of Gian Antonio Gattone?"

"Yes, close, signora."

"He writes about you with great enthusiasm. Good. What can I do for you?"

Moraldo stands up and gives a manuscript to Signora Contini. "I would like to publish something in your magazine."

Signora Contini takes the manuscript from him and looks it over. "Have you published anything elsewhere?"

"No," says Moraldo, and he swallows.

The woman looks steadily at Moraldo. His sincerity pleases her. She smiles.

"I need to find work," continues Moraldo.

"I understand."

"I have been in Rome for four months. I have looked, but things have not turned out well. I thought that with some newspapers . . . but nothing. It is hard."

"Yes, it is hard," says Signora Contini.

"Then, one day, yesterday, I saw the advertisement of your magazine, and I thought I would try here. I can do a little bit of everything, regular office work, looking after things. . . . I brought that article here, because if you like it. . . ."

Signora Contini watches him closely, without interrupting him. When he finishes, there follows an uneasy silence.

"How long have you known the poet Gattone?"

"Two weeks."

"I would like to meet him. He is an eccentric kind of writer, isn't he? It shouldn't be too hard to arrange. In the fall, I will resume giving my parties. Tell Gattone that I will see about him, I will think."

"Thank you."

"Give me time to read your article, and we'll talk about it later." While she speaks, Signora Contini gets to her feet and picks up her pocketbook. "Noon. I have to run."

Together Signora Contini and Moraldo go down the stairs. With a quick wave, they pass the doorman and enter the street, which has become hotter now that it is completely invaded by the sun.

VIII

"This heat! You just can't breathe. It's terrible to have to work in these conditions, isn't it?"

Moraldo smiles and agrees. Already he considers Signora Contini as an employer. He walks beside her with clumsy deference.

They pass in front of a cafe. "I'm thirsty," says Signora Contini. Immediately she takes a seat at a table as self-assuredly as if she were the owner, and with a curt gesture she invites Moraldo to sit across from her. She looks at him attentively. She asks again his name, which she had not completely mastered before. She asks questions about his family, the town he came from, and his studies, stopping at times to look off into the street as if she were seized by sudden, important thoughts. She mentions her magazine and the clan of artists that she has managed to promote in a short amount of time: all people of worth, professionals, some poets, and many women. Especially she talks about her favorite child, *Life and Letters*, which has required great sacrifices from her.

Moraldo listens to her with deference and at the same time tries to see out of the corner of his eye the figure on the check for the drinks. With a skillful gesture, he determines whether he has enough money in his pocket. Yes, he has even one hundred lire extra. Excellent. Meanwhile, Signora Contini is busy, too. Her stop at the bar had been strategic. She wanted to make a judgment about what kind of person this young applicant was. She finds him modest, submissive, and likeable. They could get along.

"Call me in about two weeks. I will give you some word then."

While the waiter is coming to get the money for the drinks, something happens that Moraldo did not foresee: a little flower girl puts a bouquet of flowers on the table. "Sir, won't you give these to the lady?"

Moraldo would like to destroy the girl with his glare. He tries to send her away with a gesture of his hand, but the flower girl insists, "Come on, give them to the lady. She is so pretty."

It is impossible for him to refuse. With a defeated smile,

Moraldo takes the flowers and gives his last hundred lire to the flower girl who goes off thanking him. Then he offers the flowers to Signora Contini.

"What have you done?" she says, astonished and annoyed. "You shouldn't have done that." She stands up, repeats her telephone number to Moraldo, hails a passing taxi, and rushes off to it, forgetting the flowers on the table.

Moraldo sets out on foot for his apartment. He stops at a kiosk to look at the covers of the illustrated weeklies, all of them photographs of pretty girls.

"Some stuff, eh?" says a voice behind him. Moraldo turns and discovers the man from the mezzanine who opened the door for him the night he did not have a key.

"For that one there I would be willing to spend ten years in jail," says the man from the mezzanine, indicating a pin-up girl.

Politely Moraldo agrees.

"Well, did she give you a key?"

"Yes," says Moraldo.

"Good. Don't let people walk all over you!" The man introduces himself. He is Enrico Ricci, a salesman. He is one of those outgoing Romans who show immediately their fondness for the people they like, and Moraldo is evidently one of those Ricci likes. Ricci looks at him and shakes his head as if to say, "What a guy." He smiles, winks kindly, and then asks with curiosity, "What do you do?"

"Nothing," says Moraldo.

"Journalist? Painter?"

"A little bit of everything."

After a little while, they say good-by to each other. Moraldo walks away and then turns to look back. Ricci gestures to him by shaking his head as if to allude to Moraldo's mysterious activities with sympathy and understanding.

IX

With defeat in his heart, Moraldo crosses the threshold of his room. Gattone is there, stretched out on the sofa in his pajamas, reading. "Ah, the handsome, young Moraldo," he calls. "How did it go? Did you get an advance?"

Trying to hold back his frustration, Moraldo recounts what happened: how he was received, the vague promises, and then the terrible situation at the cafe aggravated by the arrival of the flower vendor. The last of his money disappeared into thin air.

"But did my letter have an effect?"

"Yes. She says that she wants to get to know you."

"Good. The essential thing is that the letter had an effect." Satisfied, Gattone resumes reading. Then after a little while, he breaks off and asks if Moraldo has eaten lunch. Moraldo thinks it pointless to reply and maintains an injured silence.

"Ah, blessed boy," says Gattone. He gets up wearily from the sofa, leaves the apartment, and goes to the kitchen of the pension with a key. He opens the padlock on the cupboard and takes out some bread, some prosciutto, and a banana. He relocks the cupboard carefully, checks that no one has seen him, returns to the room, and gives his loot to Moraldo.

Moraldo looks at him with surprise. "Where did you get all this stuff?"

Gattone winks. "My son," he says, "can it be that you have lived in this house for three months and not discovered that the key to your suitcase can also open the padlock on the cupboard in the kitchen?" Then without savoring Moraldo's surprise too long, Gattone returns to the sofa and takes up his reading again.

X

A few days pass. In order to earn some money, Moraldo has joined forces with Lange. They have decided to paint store windows with pictures and advertising slogans. Lange has done several different sketches. They will ask a thousand lire for each window. "You will see," says Lange, "at the minimum, we will have ten thousand lire in our pockets tonight."

Moraldo does not share Lange's optimism to any great extent, but he feels the need to try something after all. For three days he has not had a regular meal.

"This evening, we will have wine, women, and song," promises Lange.

The first storeowner they approach refuses flatly to let them dirty his window. He won't discuss the matter, even for free.

"Don't worry. Rome is full of shops," Lange tells Moraldo.

A little later, they are in a shoemaker's store. There is no one else in the shop, and Lange is able to demonstrate his advertising spiel to its fullest advantage. The shoemaker listens to it with his eyes half-closed. He has no wish to speak. However, he performs an act that tips the situation to the advantage of the two friends. He looks at the sketches.

"Here, this is one that will do for your store," says Lange suddenly. He shows the owner a drawing in which a group of smiling men walk behind a curvaceous girl. Their shoes are particularly well drawn. The shoes sparkle. "The writing is done to order," says Lange.

The storeowner hesitates. "Five hundred lire," he says to get rid of the two friends.

"Very good," says Lange. He gives the sketch to Moraldo. "While you do this, I'll look for another store. There is no point in two of us working here."

Moraldo sets about the job, as ashamed as if he were a thief. He stirs for a long time the whitish mixture in the jar that Lange gave to him. He looks at his paint brush and tests it. He studies the sketch carefully. "I need a stool," he tells the storeowner.

"Please bring him a stool," the owner says to his salesgirl. It is clear that he does not trust Moraldo's abilities very far in this undertaking, but by now he wants to see how things will turn out.

Moraldo goes out into the street, sets the stool in front of the window, smiles half-heartedly at the storeowner, makes his measurements, and begins to draw a little man. The paint sticks, a good sign. He plucks up his courage and continues. The little man appears a bit oversized, but passable. Moraldo draws another one. Then he tackles the girl.

After half an hour the window is fully painted. The overall effect is clumsy, and Moraldo tries to figure out why his painting differs from the drawing.

"The figures are too big," says the owner who has followed the operation with complete distrust. "Don't you see that?"

"The bigger they are, the better they will be seen," says Moraldo.

"Well, now write, 'Grand clearance sale,'" the owner says.

Moraldo begins to write, but he gets only half the phrase on the window.

"Didn't I tell you it was too big?" says the owner, shrugging his shoulders. "The best thing now is to stop and give up."

Moraldo breaks out in a cold sweat. Around him has formed a group of people, boys, old men, and ladies who are watching him work. He is nervous. Everyone makes a comment, and unfortunately each comment bears on the ability of the painter.

Moraldo sees Lange in the process of painting a window rapidly a short distance away. He would like to call him and ask him for help, but he doesn't dare.

"Too big?" Moraldo asks the owner. The man shakes his head in contempt without answering.

"You would like the writing smaller?" hazards Moraldo.

"If you don't make it smaller, how will it fit?" says the owner. "The shoes have to be seen. If they aren't seen, how will anybody know what I sell?"

"You need to go from here to over there," says a boy.

Moraldo nods agreement, thoughtfully. He continues to sweat. "I need a rag," he says.

"Clara," calls the storeowner, "please bring this man a rag."

The salesgirl comes soon with a rag. She looks at the drawing and makes no comment.

"Some water also, please, signorina," says Moraldo.

With a very serious expression, the salesgirl returns a little later with a jar of water. Moraldo soaks the rag and rubs it over the writing to wipe it away. The paint, however, is evidently oil base.

Instead of wiping away the writing, Moraldo succeeds only in transforming it into a large smear. He gets nowhere. The more he rubs, the more he enlarges the smear.

"Good night!" says a boy. "That way now, you can't see anything."

The little group of onlookers laughs. The owner remains very somber. "What have you done now? What have you done?" he asks.

"I don't know," Moraldo answers. He continues to rub. "I'm cleaning it off now."

"You need turpentine," states an old man.

Moraldo turns to look at the person who spoke. Next to the old man, Moraldo sees a beautiful, well-groomed girl. What strikes Moraldo is that the girl is not laughing with the others. It would seem that she shares the painter's embarrassment at his inability to pull himself out of his predicament. "Yes," says the girl in a low voice, "a little bit of turpentine and it will come right off."

Moraldo thanks her with a smile.

"I'll go buy some turpentine and come back," Moraldo tells the owner. The man does not answer. He contents himself with giving Moraldo a glare of surly distrust.

While Moraldo makes his way to a store selling sundries, he passes the girl who didn't laugh at him. He stops her. "Thank you," he says to her.

The girl smiles. "For what?" she asks.

"You were very kind," he continues. "You were the only one who wasn't laughing at me." He doesn't know how to go on. He smiles. The girl smiles also. They leave each other, victims of their own shyness.

XI

It is a depressing Sunday afternoon. The streets of the Prati quarter of Rome are deserted. They reflect blazing sunlight onto the closed store fronts. Near a movie theater stands Moraldo, waiting.

"Am I late?"

Moraldo turns and greets the buxom cashier of a cafe that he frequents. She is dressed in a white outfit, her hair piled high and tinted black. She wears net gloves through which can be seen her lacquered nails. "Here I am," she says. "Where are we going?"

Moraldo links arms with her.

"No, let me be. It's too hot," the girl protests. "Tell me, where are we going?"

"Well," offers Moraldo, "I thought of going to the movies."

The girl looks at him, her eyes wide with incredulity. "To the movies! We would die of the heat!"·

"Where else then?"

"Listen, I broke at least two other dates to go out with you. I don't want to see a movie. Let's go to Ostia.[1] I've brought my bathing suit."

Distressed, Moraldo looks at her. It is clear that he does not have enough money to take the girl to Ostia. He says to her, "Ostia on Sunday? It's like a circus out there!"

"Then let's rent a little car and go to Frascati or Rocca di Papa."[2]

Moraldo brushes aside this proposal. "No, listen, let's go into the country. We'll take a trolley and have an outing."

The girl is clearly disappointed with this counterproposal. She regrets having come on this date with such a good-for-nothing. She should have known that Moraldo didn't have enough money. Wrapped in her disappointment, she remains quiet, trying to think of a way to get out of the date. "I want to go to Ostia," she repeats finally.

Moraldo is downcast. He had intended this date with the girl to be a pleasant diversion. She had seemed to him timid and

---

[1] Ostia is a beach resort on the Tyrrhenian Sea twenty miles southwest of Rome.
[2] Frascati and Rocca di Papa are historic hill towns in the Castelli Romani area, fifteen to twenty miles southeast of Rome, that have become attractions for tourists.

modest [at the shoemaker's shop],[3] but now there she was, dressed like a streetwalker, with very clear ideas about the investment of her time.

"Listen," he proposes, "why not come to my place? We'll wait for the heat to pass, and then maybe we'll go out for supper."

The girl touches her forehead with the fingers of her right hand. "What do you have for brains?" she says dryly, and then adds, "Me at your place? What a joke!"

She appears even more offended than she was previously. "If you didn't have enough money to go to Ostia, you should have said so. I work all week, and on Sunday I want to enjoy myself." She raises her voice as if he were trying to cheat her out of something.

"I'm sorry," Moraldo tries.

"What good is sorry," the girl answers. Then she makes up her mind. She puts out her hand. "It would be better if we say good-by now. I am going," she states in a loud voice.

Two young men have stopped to enjoy the scene. Moraldo squeezes the hand of the girl, who then goes off stiffly, trembling with anger. The two young men smile and jab each other with their elbows.

XII

Two hours later, Moraldo is walking on Via Cola di Rienzo, more sad and disheartened than ever. The painful solitude of the city afflicts him.

Now on the otherwise deserted pavement there moves toward him a man who holds the hand of a girl about eight years old. The man is elderly. Moraldo has met him before, but he can't remember where. When the man is nearly upon him, Moraldo

---

[3] The phrase seems to be a mistake in the manuscript. Fellini may have originally intended to use the salesgirl of Section X as Moraldo's date in this episode and failed to delete this reference when he changed to the character of the buxom cashier.

recognizes him. He is Amilcare, the waiter from the restaurant near the station. Moraldo says hello and stops. After greeting each other, neither man knows what to say. They stand facing each other awkwardly.

"You're on an outing?" Moraldo asks.

"Yes, sure, on Sundays."

"This is your daughter?"

"Yes," answers Amilcare, brightening for a moment. "Patricia, say hello to the young man."

Patricia greets Moraldo and shakes hands. Moraldo smiles and gives her a pat. He finds her very pretty and tall for her age.

"Do you go to school, Patricia?"

"Yes."

"She's in the third grade," responds the waiter proudly.

There is now an opportunity for Moraldo to end the conversation, but he hesitates to do it. On such a Sunday afternoon even the company of a man as sad as Amilcare can be precious. Unwilling to break off the conversation, Moraldo stands there looking down at the little girl.

"You don't come to the restaurant any more?" asks the waiter.

"No, but we'll be back one of these days."

Having exhausted this subject, the men fall silent again. But evidently Amilcare feels the solitude also. For him, too, Sundays are sad.

"We're going to the movies," he says finally. "If you would like to come. . . ."

"To the movies?" Moraldo considers the proposal. Then he takes the girl's free hand.

"It is on me, naturally. If you will permit me," says Amilcare.

The three of them walk along the sunny pavement.

XIII

It is evening when Moraldo comes out of the movie theater with Amilcare and the child. They are commenting on the show.

All their good will, however, has not helped them overcome the embarrassment they feel about the afternoon spent together. As Moraldo says good night to Amilcare and his daughter at the bus stop, it becomes clear that Amilcare's kind intentions were dictated more by compassion for Moraldo than by a sincere wish to make friends with him.

"Good-by, young man," says Amilcare. He has become like a waiter again.

Now Moraldo feels himself very much alone. He has managed to pass only a brief amount of time through the diversion of the movies. The evening looms ahead of him. In a short while, he will have the problems of supper and the rest of the evening to contend with. It seems enough to drive him mad. Then, almost against his will, Moraldo finds himself in a cafe telephoning Signora Contini.

The woman answers the phone herself. At first she doesn't remember who Moraldo is. Then she asks him what he wants.

"I want to talk to you."

"Is it something urgent?"

"Yes, signora, very urgent."

The woman is silent for a moment, thinking. Finally, she makes a decision. "Come to my place. But make it right away. I have to go out."

XIV

Signora Contini is alone in her apartment. She is in the process of getting ready to go out for the evening. Very sure of herself, she walks about from room to room, forcing Moraldo to follow her.

"What must you tell me that is so urgent?"

Moraldo does not know what to say now. However, he makes the effort to ask her for a loan, although it is not really money that he needs at the moment. He then begins to talk about himself, about that terrible Sunday, and about the need he felt to telephone a friendly person and to escape from the street. Perhaps, however, he acted unthinkingly and disturbed Signora Contini.

"No, no," the woman protests courteously. In her eyes, nevertheless, there is a glint of coldness.

"You told me to phone you, and I didn't know where else to turn. This Sunday is the problem. But now I won't disturb you any more."

"I understand," says Signora Contini, looking at Moraldo. She has become serious. She, too, has experienced such moments. She experiences them still, those moments when she feels the earth about to tumble down on her. Solitude, what a great and terrible thing it is! She longs for it so much, but then, when it comes, it kills. All that afternoon she shut herself up in her apartment. She tried to "knock off" some pages of her novel, but finally she had to give up. She didn't feel sincere, and for a writer sincerity is everything.

"Get a grip on yourself. You're very young."

Sitting down, Signora Contini crosses her legs. Moraldo looks at her. Her legs are long and shapely. Her dressing gown reaches only to the top of her knees. Suddenly Moraldo feels desire for this woman. His look becomes slightly hard and insistent. Signora Contini notices his look and touches the edge of her dressing gown lightly with her hand.

"What are your plans for the evening?" she asks.

Moraldo shrugs. He has no plans. He is alone, desperate. Knowingly, he plays out his role in the comedy. He wishes to see the situation through to its conclusion.

"It's a shame that I have an engagement," says Signora Contini. "People whom you don't know." But the young man pleases her. She has already made a judgment about him. He suits her. She gets up, runs a hand through her hair, and marches decisively into her bedroom.

"Would you mind waiting for me while I finish getting dressed?"

"No, signora."

Signora Contini begins putting on her stockings while singing softly. She bumps the lamp on the night table, and the light goes out. A short circuit.

"Oh! What now!" she cries.

Moraldo offers to fix the problem. He goes into the kitchen, takes equipment from a drawer, and removes the burnt fuse from its socket, while the woman admires his ability in the matter. After a little while, the light comes back on.

"Very well done!" applauds Signora Contini. She seizes Moraldo's arm suddenly. "Listen, I have an idea. I'll call my friends and tell them I'll be a little late. I hate to see you looking so sad." While she is telephoning, she takes Moraldo's hand and squeezes it as a sign of interest.

She hangs up the receiver. "See," she says, "you make me tell lies for you." She smiles and shakes her finger at him. Then because he seems melancholy still, she adds, "Come on! Don't be so sad! I always try to fight back." She thinks for a moment, shakes her head, and sighs vigorously. "Yes, one always has to fight back."

Signora Contini looks Moraldo squarely in the eyes. She sits on the bed and poses as a woman who has experienced all there is to experience in life. "Little boy," she murmurs.

In an instant Moraldo is beside her. He embraces her, and she allows herself to be embraced. She arches up her breasts and flares her nostrils dramatically. "No, no. Are you mad?" she says, while she searches for the switch to the lamp with her hand.

XV

Two hours later, Moraldo is in the bathroom combing his hair and splashing on cologne. He finds a shaving brush on the shelf and asks himself what possible use Signora Contini could have for it. There is also a razor on the shelf. Probably a man turns up by chance every now and then.

A noise from the entrance hall distracts him from these thoughts. Who has come in?

"Someone is here, signora," Moraldo says to the woman who now appears in the doorway to the bedroom. She is in her dressing gown and is in the process of doing her nails.

"It's only the maid," she tells him. Evidently Signora Contini places no importance on the fact that the maid will discover him in shirt sleeves. And in fact, when the maid sees Moraldo, she does not seem surprised. She gives him a courteous, simple greeting.

"Good evening, signora," the maid says in a loud voice.

"Hello, Lina. I'm not eating here tonight. Just fix something for yourself," says Signora Contini. Then she turns back to Moraldo and says, "I'm going to join my friends. You're on your way, aren't you?"

Now that Signora Contini has regained control of herself and again thinks of herself as the directress of a publication, she wants to reestablish a certain distance. But, on the other hand, she likes the young man and doesn't want to put him off with behavior that is too cold. "Let's get together again on Wednesday," she suggests. "Phone me first, around breakfast time."

Moraldo agrees. He feels shy and awkward. He is not able to use the familiar form *tu* with a woman he held in his arms just a short time ago. Moraldo makes his way out, but before he leaves the apartment he gives a final glance at the stacks of *Life and Letters* that surround the door. He is not very pleased with himself now. He realizes, though, that the Sunday is over and that it has turned out better than he had thought it would. Perhaps he would be happier if the maid were not accompanying him to the door, silently, watching him with a certain air of scorn.

XVI

A week has passed. Moraldo has seen Signora Contini again. However, he has not spoken to his friends about his adventures with her.

Gattone is still his roommate. Gattone has managed to convince the landlady that he will pay rent at the end of two weeks without fail. He is a likeable person, and he knows how to put to good use his long experience with landladies. He has praised the landlady's deceased husband, and he has performed odd jobs for her. Leisure time and frugal but regular meals have improved his appearance. Now he is always full of ideas. And he steals regularly from the cupboard in the landlady's kitchen. To Moraldo who worries that they will be caught, Gattone says simply, "We have to survive, my good friend."

On this particular day, Gattone has stolen half a cold chicken. He and Moraldo are in the act of eating it in silence when the landlady enters the room without knocking. Surprised, both men sit there, each with a piece of chicken in his hands.

At first the landlady says nothing. She strides to the center of the room, staring at her chicken in someone else's hands, and she nods her head, feigning pleasure. "Ah, good, good." Then abruptly she explodes. "Thieves! Robbers! Crooks! Get out of my house at once, or I'll report you to the police!"

Moraldo tries to protest, although he can find no grounds that sound convincing even to him. With a swat, the landlady knocks the piece of chicken from his hands.

"Quiet, you, or you'll end up behind bars," she tells him.

Hurrying to finish his piece of chicken, Gattone speaks with his mouth full. He tries to explain that the situation is a misunderstanding and that he thought the chicken belonged to Moraldo.

The cries of the landlady draw the other tenants. The situation has become serious, and even Gattone, with all his diplomatic ability, cannot control it.

"Get out at once, or else I'll telephone the police. You thieves! You robbers! I'll give you ten minutes to get out of my building," she shouts. "For two weeks now they have been stealing from my kitchen, those two."

All the rancor she has built up against Moraldo for his evasions

of her veiled, amorous proposals now explodes in a torrent of vul-
garities. In order to quiet her, Moraldo gets his suitcase and
begins to put his things into it. Gattone, who has nothing of his
own to pack, helps Moraldo. "Calm down. We're going," says
Gattone. "This is no way to treat two gentlemen, on the basis of
unfounded suspicions."

XVII

Now the two men have the problem of where to go. Gattone,
however, solves the problem immediately by hailing a cab and
giving the driver the address of the Savoy Hotel. To Moraldo who
gapes at him, Gattone explains, "Drastic situations call for drastic
solutions, my good friend. We will spend a day or two at the
Savoy. We will take our meals in the room. The doorman will pay
the cabdriver. And then something will turn up. Don't you
agree?"

Moraldo doesn't agree at all, but Gattone seems so sure of
himself that Moraldo doesn't object. In a way, the idea of going to
the Savoy Hotel appeals to Moraldo.

Half an hour later, they are installed in a magnificent room
with twin beds and a bath. Having taken a shower and ordered
some chilled wine, Gattone is a completely happy man. By telephone Gattone and Moraldo have summoned Lange to the room
for a council of war. He approves of their maneuver but makes it
clear that he has no money to lend them. The business of painting
the shop windows ended after two days. The month has not been
propitious for business ventures.

"What you need is a sizeable loan. But how in the world
would that be possible?" says Lange.

"It is always easier to get a loan for a large amount of money
than it is for a small amount," states Gattone sententiously.

"I agree with you in theory," says Lange. "But we're in
August now. Right in the middle of vacation time. Everyone is
out of town."

"Let's make a list of friends," suggests Gattone.

Lange picks up a pencil and starts a list. At the third name he stops. "This is a lot of trouble to go to," he says. Then he adds, "First let's make an estimate of how much money you need."

The estimate is soon done. Two days in the hotel, four meals, taxi, tips, et cetera: not less than fifteen thousand lire. Who would lend fifteen thousand lire to two loafers like them? Slowly the specters of scandal and prison loom up before their eyes. The situation is grave.

"You know what you do in a situation like this?" asks Gattone. "You order another bottle sent up, and maybe you telephone a couple of girls."

Moraldo and Lange have no desire to laugh. A waiter enters and delivers sandwiches ordered by Gattone.

"Nothing but the best in this hotel, eh?" says Gattone. The waiter is very reserved. He gives the three of them a glance that says it all. He has sized them up as deadbeats. When he leaves, our friends feel put down.

Lange wants to emphasize that he is not in the same fix as the other two. "Well, you'll find a way to get out of this," he says. "Sorry I have to go."

"I could write home," volunteers Moraldo. Immediately he regrets what he has said. "No, not home, never that!" When he left home, he made himself a solemn promise that he would never ask for a penny. But he had to go back on that promise once already when he contacted his mother secretly. Now he doesn't have the gall to write a letter scrounging for money again.

"Well, what then?" asks Gattone. He has no money coming to him, only debts to pay. His collaborations . . . .

"Wait a moment!" exclaims Gattone, turning to Moraldo. "There's always your article. Signora Contini has accepted it, hasn't she?"

Moraldo admits that Signora Contini seems to have accepted the article. The journal, though, has not come out yet. He cannot ask for an advance for anything as large as they need.

"What scruples!" says Lange. "Everyone asks for advances. Signora Contini will understand."

Moraldo defends his position. Then, finally, to stop his friends, he intimates that something is going on between Signora Contini and him. He can't appeal to her for money. Gattone stops arguing, but Lange cries that it is madness not to use someone who is so well disposed to Moraldo. Lange would not hesitate a minute. He encourages Moraldo to speak frankly with Signora Contini. "If she really likes you, she will understand."

Gattone remains silent. The matter is delicate. He wants to leave the decision to Moraldo. Lange is at the telephone. "What is the number of Signora Contini?"

Moraldo gives him the number, and Lange repeats it to the telephone operator.

XVIII

"Well, then?" asks Signora Contini. They are in her study. Moraldo is seated in an easy chair in front of her. He does not know how to start.

"My article. . .," he begins and then stops.

"Your article. Ah, yes! I have read it."

"I would like to know. . . . Are you going to publish it?"

"Yes, I think so. Only, I don't know, you see, if it will be in the next issue. It's almost completely laid out already."

Moraldo looks at the floor. He summons up his courage and says, "But you are going to publish it?"

"Yes, darling, certainly."

"Well, then. . . . Excuse me, you know, it is very difficult to. . . ."

"What is the matter?" Signora Contini's curiosity is aroused. Moraldo recounts everything to her. He tells her of his urgent need for money and of his hope of getting an advance from her on the article he submitted. Then he becomes confused and starts his speech again from the beginning, apologizing profusely.

"How much do you need?" Signora Contini interrupts him sweetly. Then since Moraldo hesitates to answer, she suggests, "Twenty thousand?"

Moraldo hangs his head. "Yes."

Signora Contini calls the maid and gives her a key. "Darling, go and bring my pocketbook from the chest of drawers."

The maid leaves the room. There is a long silence. Finally, Signora Contini asks, "Where do you intend to go now?"

"I don't know. I'll find another room."

The woman thinks for a moment. "You could stay here for a few days."

"Here?"

"I could make up the little room over there for you. Would you like that?"

The proposal is all too clear. Signora Contini is not paying an advance on the article; she is giving him money in order to make Moraldo understand that their relationship has now changed. There is no point in being crude: let us say simply that Signora Contini wishes to help the young man.

The maid returns with the pocketbook. She does not look at Moraldo. Signora Contini takes out two bills, ten thousand lire each, from the pocketbook.

"Shouldn't I sign a receipt, for the records?" asks Moraldo timidly.

"No. It's not necessary. This is my money, not the journal's," states the woman. Then she adds, "You can move in this evening. Is that all right? There's no sense in spending more money at the hotel. Especially since it's my money that's being spent."

Moraldo takes the money. To underline further the implications of the gift, Signora Contini gives him a caress.

"Well, then," she says, "set your affairs in order and come back as soon as possible. I'll be waiting for you." She has assumed again the commanding tone of a directress.

XIX

Leaving the apartment building, Moraldo feels exhausted. He didn't think that matters would become so complicated or that he would have to enter into such a bargain.

Suddenly a little, beat-up black Fiat slams to a stop nearby. Someone calls Moraldo. In order to see who it is, Moraldo has to go up to the car and peer through the windshield.

Seated behind the wheel of the car is Enrico Ricci, the tenant from the mezzanine. He is smiling, happy to see Moraldo again. As always, he is mysteriously elusive behind his constant smiles, and, as always, he is full of warmth, human kindness, and sympathy.

"Tell me what you're up to."

"Nothing much," answers Moraldo evasively.

Ricci's car is filled with stationery items. He is selling them.

"Can you use any carbon paper?" he asks.

"No," Moraldo thanks him. He can't think of a way to end the conversation.

Laboriously Ricci climbs out of the little car. The two men go for coffee together.

Ricci is filled with the joy of being alive. He insists on paying for the coffee and urges Moraldo to order something to eat. Smiling, he watches Moraldo. He seems very pleased with the chance encounter. "I'm often away from Rome now. I work hard," he says. Then he gives Moraldo his phone number. "In case you need me sometime in the future."

Moraldo thanks him.

A little later, Moraldo enters the hotel and settles the bill. He divides the money left over between Gattone and himself. Then he says good-by.

"I'm going to stay with some friends of my father for a few days."

Gattone is not happy to separate from Moraldo. Now he will feel all the more alone. Yet he is cheered by the few thousand lire Moraldo has given him. The money makes him certain that tomorrow will be a fine day and that things will work out well.

XX

So it is that Moraldo enters into an "arrangement" with the "old broad," as Lange puts it. Everything considered, Lange is a little envious of his friend's sexual luck. Yes, it is a veritable "arrangement." In exchange for his food and lodging, Signora Contini has Moraldo perform a little bit of work at the office, odd jobs only, and reserves his major efforts for the bedroom. Moraldo doesn't have the strength any longer to consider what he is doing. He allows himself to be carried along. One day he accepts a cigarette lighter, the next day a necktie, and the day after that a small reprimand in front of the maid.

One evening returning home unexpectedly, Moraldo finds another young man in the study. He is a robust, lifeguard type. Signora Contini introduces the young man to Moraldo as a writer, but the young man glares at Moraldo with a certain air of rivalry. When Signora Contini shows the young man out, she lingers at the door slightly longer than is necessary.

"Who was that guy?" Moraldo asks later at supper.

"A friend."

"A friend?" Moraldo questions ironically.

"Darling," says Signora Contini dryly, "I do not grant you the right to pass judgments on the friends I want to have around me. Is that understood?"

Moraldo falls silent. Later that evening while washing the dishes, the maid sings triumphantly.

XXI

The living room, the study, and the entrance hall of the Contini apartment are full of guests.

"*Commendatore*, my good friend!"[4]

"*Maestro!*"

---

[4]*Commendatore* is an honorary title given for civil merit, usually accorded to important men of business.

"Ah, Signora Bellotti, you know you are a love."

"You must not say such things to me, counselor."

To celebrate the publication of the second issue of *Life and Letters*, Signora Contini has decided to open her salon again. By now the hot spell has ended, and all her friends have returned to the city. On a Sunday afternoon she gives a cocktail party for *Life and Letters*. She has invited the Friends of Noah's Ark, a literary society of which she is a charter member.

For the occasion, Moraldo wears a new blue suit, a gift from Signora Contini. He supervises the laying out of the buffet. Signora Contini has engaged a well-known pastry shop of Prati to do things well. They have sent a waiter in a white jacket.

Crowds of guests invade the office, the entrance hall, the living room, and even the bedroom. Signora Contini is made up like a diva. She wears a black velvet dress trimmed with lace. Moving happily from group to group, she distributes overly wide smiles, handshakes, and even some kisses.

We look over the guests. All are older than forty. The women wearing their little hats are fat and self-indulgent, habitual eaters of cream-filled delicacies. The men are "artistic," a little bald, and with paunches, or else tall lawyers with leonine manes of hair. All are "into literature." Some have written, and some think about writing. Some give lectures, and others are knowledgeable about music.

"I tell you, he is a phenomenal talent. Another Picasso."

"And then you didn't send me a copy of your book. What am I to think of that!"

"Listen to this one. A man from Milan. . . ."

The cocktail party goes on with great animation. Everyone drinks and talks. After a little while, the women begin to lose their inhibitions.

"No, counselor, this joke is for women only."

"Well then, he. . . ." Everyone laughs.

"This is terrible. But do you know the one about the major-domo?"

The more serious men talk about simple, everyday things.

"Yes, but the Alfa Romeo has more pick-up."

"You can fit five people in easily, and then if a chance for a little hanky-panky should come along. . . ."

Moraldo moves from one cluster of people to another, without staying long with any one group. He thinks it unlikely he will find rapport with anyone at the party, but he looks, nevertheless, for a face he could call friendly. His surprise is enormous when from the door of the entry hall he sees Gattone walk through the front door. Gattone is as happy as a schoolboy on vacation.

"Gattone!" The two men embrace each other.

"I got an invitation. I knew you would be here. And so I came."

Yes, Signora Contini sent an invitation to Gattone. For the occasion he has shaved and has gotten a haircut, and he has put on a clean shirt. Gattone looks like a different person. At once he declares his wish to become roaringly drunk. His entrance has caused a stir among the other guests. At last, someone who seems to be an earthy, eccentric artist! Signora Contini is delighted with his arrival. Moraldo, on the other hand, is somewhat embarrassed to be caught in his job as "male secretary" to Signora Contini.

After a quarter of an hour, Gattone is a little bit tipsy, and he begins to shock the ladies with his pronouncements. But they let him go on. He is so amusing. Finally, Gattone takes Moraldo aside, and with an air of great secrecy he whispers, "You're doing well here, aren't you?"

"Please. . . ."

"I like your Signora Contini. She must make love very well."

Signora Contini comes up on them unexpectedly. "What is our poet saying?"

"Not much. I was just saying to Moraldo that you. . . ."

"Please don't!" interrupts Moraldo.

"What's wrong? I was just telling him that you are a very capable woman. Yes, well . . . I think we understand each other." Gattone winks and bursts out in a raucous laugh.

Signora Contini gives a hollow laugh and moves away.

Moraldo leaves Gattone and goes to get a whiskey. He drinks

in order to get rid of his anger. He overhears a conversation from a group near him.

"Have you seen Signora Contini's boy?"

"A nice-looking kid."

"Yes, but I don't envy him his job. He'll have to work long hours for that one."

Moraldo moves away from the group. Two women in the middle of an animated conversation see him approach and stop talking. They seem slightly embarrassed. They smile at Moraldo, and he walks on.

A lawyer with a leonine mane of hair insists on offering Moraldo a toast. The lawyer wants to ingratiate himself with Signora Contini. Moraldo feels on edge. He goes into the hallway to get away from the people, but everywhere he goes he feels that the guests are talking about him and making cracks about his "good luck."

Signora Contini joins him. "You aren't bored, are you?"

"No, not at all."

"Well, please try not to be so surly with my friends. You ought to make them like you and take an interest in you. It's very important to your career."

"Yes."

"Do you know what I think? That next Saturday we'll go to Taormina for a week. Does that please you? There's a conference, and I'll take you with me. It will be beautiful. But you have to deserve the trip." Having made her point, Signora Contini gives Moraldo a rapid caress and walks away.

The cocktail party continues. In the bedroom of Signora Contini, a group of men and women talk in a lively way. When one of the men sees Moraldo come in, he coughs. The others keep on talking, but in too jovial a manner. Moraldo leaves the bedroom and feels a burst of laughter explode behind him.

XXII

Two hours later, the cocktail party nears its conclusion. Many of the guests have left. The maid has great trouble retrieving coats from the various heaps in her room.

Gattone has not behaved well. In addition to having become too drunk to stand up, he has begun a long, confused conversation with the buffet attendant on the subject of how champagne is made and bottled. To illustrate his thesis, he asks that another bottle be uncorked.

"That's your third," says the attendant.

"Excuse me, my friend, but why does that bother you? Do you manage the business affairs of the hostess? We're having a literary reception here. Uncork the bottle!"

Even when the last of the other guests has gone, Gattone continues his conversation cheerfully by himself, stretched out on the sofa.

Now there remains only the sad task of cleaning up after the party. The buffet must be cleared away, the rooms straightened up, the ashtrays emptied, and the glasses fished out from under the furniture. The maid, urged on by Signora Contini, does her best, but she is exhausted almost to the breaking point. She grumbles and shoves the furniture around brusquely.

Moraldo decides to help her, but, before he can begin, the maid drops a tray, and the glasses on it shatter into a thousand pieces.

"Damnit to hell," says Moraldo. His suit has been stained.

"It isn't my fault," the maid cries.

"I didn't say it was," Moraldo tells her.

The maid, however, has passed her breaking point. "I do what I can," she yells. "Why don't you ever do anything? After all, you're one of the paid help, too!"

Brought into the room by the uproar, Signora Contini intervenes. She asks Moraldo what happened. Reluctantly he tells her about it. She becomes angry. "So now you pick fights with the maid!"

"But I didn't say anything to her."

"All right, all right, but remember this. I value Lina very

highly. She does her job well. She's loyal. And she doesn't steal."
Signora Contini goes off solemnly to hear Lina's side of the story.

Moraldo is filled with self-contempt. He glances around him.
He looks at his new suit. It seems to him that he has struck bottom. The comments of the guests, the scorn of the maid, and even
Gattone's attitude about his situation have all served to destroy
his self-delusions and to make him realize what he has become, a
little gigolo, a domestic servant who has to ask for pocket money.
He could stay in this condition for a long time, as long as Signora
Contini doesn't get tired of him. But suppose he himself should
get tired of things and take off? . . . It is too much to expect of life
to think that the way to attain goals should be so comfortable. He did not come to Rome to be kept by an older woman.
Gattone, dozing on the sofa, is a thousand times a better man
than he is, even if Gattone has debts, misses meals, and sleeps in
doorways.

Moraldo shakes Gattone. "Come on. Let's go."

"Go?"

"Let's get some air. It'll do us good."

He drags Gattone to the door. Signora Contini calls to
Moraldo. Since Gattone is present, she uses the formal manner of
address. "You will be back soon, won't you, Moraldo?"

"Yes, signora."

Moraldo opens the door and goes down the stairs, struggling
to keep Gattone on his feet. When he comes to the main door of
the building, Moraldo stops and searches through his pockets.
He finds his keys and gives them to the doorman. "Here," he
says, "give these back to Signora Contini. I still have a suitcase up
there. If she'll turn it over to you, I'll come by and get it."

Moraldo and Gattone leave the building. The doorman, who
finally understands, looks at the keys and smiles to himself. At
last he has something interesting to tell the tenants.

PART TWO

XXIII

In the period that follows, circumstances throw Moraldo together with Enrico Ricci. Gattone has vanished on one of his customary, unexplained absences. Lange works in another part of the city. Probably Lange continues to eat in his usual restaurant, but Moraldo no longer eats there himself. In Rome, all you have to do to lose touch with a circle of friends is to change restaurants or cafes.

Now Moraldo moves in the orbit of Ricci, the cafes, the restaurants, and the sections Ricci frequents. He meets Ricci's friends, people with worn-out shoes, with fingers black from nicotine, with immeasurably long nails on their little fingers, with good-luck charms on their wrists or in their watchpockets, and with dirty collars on their shirts despite the pretense of quality in their choices of suits. They are people always on the move, always with their ears pricked up, full of winks, rapid, fast nods of comprehension, and quick, continual calls made from public telephone booths. They are people who spend their lives trying everything, no matter how far-fetched, to make the big strike and never manage to pull it off.

Their inexhaustible capacity to struggle and their stubborn will to survive attract Moraldo, maybe even more than the opportunity of making money with them does. Ricci has made him a partner in a business venture, and the two work together. The venture is a change from Ricci's norm. It is work on consignment. Profits are uncertain. The job consists of selling several thousand memorandum books put out by a charitable institution. For each copy sold, the two salesmen will make a commission that they will divide in two parts, unequal, but fair. Moraldo will get one-third, and Ricci two-thirds. Ricci, however, will contribute the use of his beat-up little Fiat.

The selling of these memorandum books is not an easy task. The salesman has to enter stores and offices and overcome the hostilities and suspicions of the customers. Very often he won't succeed. Ricci is brazen and very experienced. Moraldo has neither of these qualities, but he tries to do what he can.

Toward the end of a very tiring day, Moraldo is in the process of trying to sell one of the memorandum books to the owner of a grocery store. He repeats for the one-hundreth time his sales-pitch, trying to be relaxed and yet persuasive. The owner listens in silence with a surly look on his face. A customer enters the store, and the owner moves away from Moraldo without giving him a yes or no. "Be back in a minute," he grunts. Moraldo interprets this response as favorable and waits patiently. When the customer leaves, Moraldo plunges on with his salespitch with a smile on his face. The owner allows him to repeat the innumerable uses of the memorandum book, and then, when Moraldo finishes, the owner asks him in an aggressive, needling tone, "What are you in here for, anyway?"

Moraldo realizes there is no use in continuing, and he walks out of the store without another word.

It's evening. A few blocks away, Ricci waits for Moraldo near his little black Fiat overloaded with memorandum books. Moraldo walks toward him very slowly. For both of them, it is enough to see the face of the other to know that things have not gone well. Moraldo is tired and discouraged. Ricci makes no comment, not even to himself. He has had days worse than this before.

Standing on the corner, they add up the totals for the day. So much for Moraldo. So much for Ricci. Good-by. See you tomorrow.

"Tomorrow," says Ricci, "we'll go to another section. This one is lousy. We'll go to one where there's more business, and the people listen to you. We'll unload at least a hundred."

XXIV

Ricci's Fiat moves away with a clanking of metal, leaving Moraldo by himself with only a few lire in his pockets. At this hour, when the neon lights come on everywhere and the crowd gets thicker and moves faster, Moraldo feels his loneliness weigh heavily on him. And his poverty as well. The faces of the people around him seem hostile and foreign. They fill him with dismay.

He walks slowly toward home from one street to another, feeling sad and lost. Discouraged, he doesn't see anything in his future.

Finally he decides to enter a small, inexpensive restaurant. In spite of everything, he is hungry. Moraldo takes a seat at a table and orders rice croquettes and a quarter liter of wine. His finances don't permit anything more. The restaurant is one he has never been to before, in a quarter almost completely unknown to him. Around him is a sea of strange faces. The buzzing of voices makes him dizzy. Suddenly among the faces, Moraldo recognizes one. At another table a girl is smiling at him. Moraldo nods hello to her. It is the girl he met when he was trying to paint the shop window. Now she is with a girl friend and two young men, maybe co-workers who decided to stop off in the little place for half an hour on the way home. After the greeting, the girl does not look back at Moraldo until the moment when her group passes in front of him on their way out. Then she smiles at him for a second time. After she is gone, Moraldo sits at his table feeling very much by himself.

Moraldo, in turn, pays and leaves the restaurant. He does not know where to go or what to do. Ahead of him is only the prospect of a bleak, solitary walk through the nocturnal city, waiting for sleepiness to force him back into his rented room.

Moraldo strolls idly by store windows that have been dark for a long time now. Perhaps his thoughts are going back with involuntary nostalgia to his hometown in the provinces and to evenings spent there with his friends.

Suddenly, near a trolley stop, he sees the girl again. Now she is alone. She stands there staring off into space, waiting for the trolley. She is not aware that Moraldo is approaching. He calls to her, "Signorina, hello."

The girl turns. As Moraldo did a few moments earlier, she gives a surprised and pleased little jump.

"You're by yourself?" Moraldo asks.

"Yes, I'm on my way home."

"Me too."

They talk to each other with an unexpected naturalness, as if they were old friends. "Do you live in this quarter?" she asks.

"No, in Prati. I'm just here by chance. You?"

"Oh, I live a long way from here, toward the Piazza Bologna. It's very inconvenient for work, but what can you do?"

"You work near here?"

"I'm a clerk at Necchi's. I got tired of having to ask my father for money all the time. Now at least I make enough for an occasional movie. And you, what are you doing? Still painting store windows?"

The girl laughs. Moraldo laughs, too, but he also blushes. It's not so much because of the business of the store window as it is the idea of explaining his current job to her. He sticks to generalities, and he lies. Moraldo tells her he has an excellent position with a first-rate agency. Evidently he wants to cut an imposing figure for this girl whose name, he realizes, he doesn't know.

"What's your name?"

"Andreina. What's yours?"

"Moraldo."

Both of them are a little excited. In a brief space of time they have gotten to know a great deal about each other. The solitude that had weighed heavily on them in the middle of the nocturnal city has now become welcome. The idea of going home seems simply absurd at this moment.

"Why don't we go to a movie?" proposes Moraldo.

The girl accepts immediately. Certainly. Why not? First she

must call home so that her mother and father won't worry. Meanwhile Moraldo buys a newspaper. He looks over the entertainment page, makes some choices, and proposes them. They agree on a film and smile at each other. The evening that began gloomily with discouragement and depression in the air has suddenly become exciting, joyful, and happy. Around them, the crowd no longer seems threatening, and the neon lights in the street are no longer menacing.

Moraldo takes Andreina's arm. They go off together at a rapid pace, chattering nonstop, among the people.

XXV

A monsignor, an industrialist, and a *commendatore*. Moraldo has consulted an old list of addresses, recommendations supplied him by his father. He decided to put the list to use. Resolutely he threw himself into the task of finding a serious job. Enough with adventure. Enough with chronic poverty that saps initiative and drains hope.

The monsignor received Moraldo in his apartment in old Rome, offered him coffee politely, inquired carefully about Moraldo's principles and activities, and gave him some vague promises. The industrialist had told Moraldo to call at another time. The *commendatore*, however, was better disposed to Moraldo. He invited Moraldo to supper one evening. The invitation couldn't have come at a better time, because for several days, despite Moraldo's best efforts, his dinners had been little more than sham rituals. He had given up the impossible-to-sell memorandum books. Ricci had dedicated himself to selling a shipment of ladies' underwear and a consignment of carbon paper and then had vanished into the provinces on a trip.

Now on the evening of the supper with the *commendatore*, however, Moraldo lingers with Andreina. Then he realizes that he has forgotten the exact address of the *commendatore*. For a long while, he wanders through unfamiliar streets, even ringing the bell at an apartment [of some gypsies][5] by mistake. Finally full of anxiety and dying of hunger, he manages to arrive at the right door. But he is so late that the *commendatore* and his family have already finished supper. To save face, Moraldo is forced to say that he thought the invitation was for after dinner and that he has already eaten.

"At least have some coffee with us," exclaims the *commendatore*, and he leads the way back to the table. The aroma of the food is still in the air of the elegant and comfortable room. Moraldo hears the sounds of plates and crockery. With an empty feeling in his stomach, he drinks the coffee. Thank goodness that the *commendatore* seems seriously interested in him.

"Leave it to me. I'll think of something. Young men of good will deserve to be helped." The *commendatore* jots down Moraldo's address.

The fact is that something new is happening in Moraldo's life. The unusual energy he bustles about with now is proof of this fact.

The new element is Andreina. After the first meeting, Moraldo has continued to see her almost every night. The evening date with her has become a regular thing for Moraldo almost without his realizing it. Andreina is fresh, lively, and serene. She belongs to a well-to-do family. Her father is an insurance agent. Everything about her reveals her background. She has a certain innate security, good, sound common sense, and an optimism that comes from the absence of serious problems—all the things Moraldo lacks.

At the beginning, Moraldo thought it very natural to alternate dates with Andreina with dates with other girls such as a cashier from a bar or a salesgirl from a store—girls met by chance. But gradually the dates with others began to annoy Moraldo, and, without her knowing it, Andreina became the only woman

---

[5] Printed here in the 1954 Italian version is the typographical error "tsareni." As best Fellini could remember in 1978, the word he intended was "zingari" (gypsies).

in his life. Then one day, finally, she came to Moraldo's room and became his lover, with naturalness, without asking anything of him, as if it were something understood between them for a long time.

XXVI

Stretched out on his bed, Moraldo listens off and on to the incessant chattering of Andreina as she finishes getting dressed. Their relationship has gone on now for almost a month, and Andreina feels very much at home in Moraldo's room. Moraldo enjoys watching her move around the room, straightening up the furniture and picking up his clothes. Andreina is a beautiful girl, and her presence delights Moraldo. He does not, however, always listen to her conversations through to the end. She talks at length about her co-workers whom Moraldo does not know, about her girl friends whom Moraldo does not know, and about her parents whom Moraldo does not know. And she speaks about these people in great detail as if Moraldo did know them and was concerned to hear about everything related to them. Her remarks sometimes make Moraldo smile, but his smiles are ones of tenderness for the solid common sense in the statements. Her voice is pleasing.

This evening, however, Moraldo feels suddenly the desire to see his old friends Gattone and Lange again. He has heard nothing about them for a long while. Suppose he went to look for them in the usual restaurant where they ate? And suppose he took Andreina with him? For a moment, the thought of exposing Andreina to aspects of his former life gives him some uneasiness, but he soon gets over it. Andreina agrees immediately to the proposal. Such is always the case with her. She likes unexpected adventures.

Andreina makes her customary telephone call home. "Please have dinner without me. I'll be late. Some extra work. I'll get something on the way home. Good night."

With the little white lie behind them, they happily go out arm-in-arm, to encounter the events of the evening.

XXVII

In the restaurant they find only Lange. He is seated by himself at a table. He greets Moraldo as if he had seen him only the day before.

Moraldo introduces Andreina to Lange. "My fiancée," Moraldo adds, after a slight hesitation.

Evidently Lange has a casual definition of the term fiancée, because he shows little reaction. He does not ask for explanatory details or offer congratulations. Without further ado, he addresses Andreina in the familiar form of address. His treatment of her puzzles Andreina. In addition, the artist launches into a series of scabrous arguments in his usual language with no holds barred, delivered at great speed.

In the past all this would have seemed completely natural to Moraldo. Now, however, he feels uneasy. He tries to change the subject. He asks for news about Gattone. The result is that things get worse.

"Yes, he is back here. He turns up every now and then. But do you know what that animal did? He ran off with a sixteen-year-old girl for a while. A fresh, young girl with nice little tits. I don't know what got into the head of that little whore to make her take up with Gattone. They almost ended up behind bars, the two of them."

Moraldo squirms in his seat and shoots guarded, worried looks at Andreina. She concentrates on her meal and pretends not to pay attention to what Lange is talking about. Meanwhile, the voluble Lange moves onto a different topic. He unrolls a large sheet of paper and displays a sketch done in bold, strong lines.

"It's Salomons, the soccer player. He comes here almost every evening. I've been sketching him without his knowing it. This evening I'm going to finish it and palm it off on him. I need to give a little money to the owner here. He hasn't seen anything from me in two months."

Each time she has to order a course during the conversation, Andreina looks uncomfortable, as if she were afraid the waiter would take her for a friend of Lange.

Suddenly the door bangs open, and in walks Gattone. He strides into the middle of the room, with his dirty raincoat open and flying out behind him, his face beet-red, rolling his r's as he speaks in a loud voice. Following him is a girl about six feet tall, thin, blondish, and unhappy looking. Gattone's greetings are loud and effusive. He hugs Moraldo, bends to kiss the hand of Andreina like a gentleman, and pays her a compliment in the witty style of the literary world. Then he introduces the beanpole with him as "little Hilda." He draws up a chair for her and helps her off with her coat as if she were a great lady.

"Thank you," says the blond in a mournful, Teutonic accent. She begins at once to devour some pieces of bread without saying anything else for a long time.

Gattone is obviously tipsy. You can smell the wine on his breath. But he holds his drink well. He orders a liter of wine, and then another one. He eats avidly, commenting as usual on the food in his Salgarian slang.[6] "This chicken is excellent, but it is clearly inferior to the meat of the iguana. . . . Innkeeper, you rogue, give us another liter." When something does not suit him, he bangs his fist on the table and shouts in a melodramatic tone: "By God, you don't know how to serve gentlemen. . . . Grooms from the stables are the only customers you deserve, by God!"

Everyone in the restaurant turns to look at him. They are astonished and a little frightened. Andreina blushes. She wants to disappear. The others at the table, though, hardly raise an eyebrow. Little Hilda chews away on her food, without talking, devouring unbelievable quantities.

"Eat, darling, eat," Gattone encourages her at intervals, although his urging seems unnecessary.

---

[6] The reference is to the Italian novelist Emilio Salgari (1862-1911), a writer of swashbuckling adventure stories.

As for Lange, he is completely absorbed in finishing his sketch of the soccer star who has entered the room surrounded by his retinue of fans.

Next Gattone recounts his adventures with "little Laura," the sixteen-year-old. He alternates between talking about the intimate details of the affair and discussing the dangers to his personal well-being that he incurred. "Her father is a cretin. He refused to understand. He wanted to report me. Me, can you imagine that!" Gattone guffaws, his face purple with wry glee. "I had to make a run for it. I fled to Algiers." How he was able to get to Algiers, Gattone does not divulge, but he concludes, "Disgusting country, Algiers. Continous diarrhea. But I wrote some very beautiful lyrics there. Maybe someone will publish them for me now, who knows?"

Gattone pours himself more to drink. Tiredly, little Hilda continues to eat. Her glassy eyes are fixed on Andreina. Finally in her terrible Italo-German slang, she says to Andreina, "I want to introduce you to my sugar daddy. Very good. Much money."

Now Lange rises to his feet. He winks at Moraldo and strolls idly toward the table of sports people. He introduces himself and shows them the sketch. The young men look at it suspiciously as they pass it around. One of them makes a joke about it. The soccer star himself looks at it for a long time, and then he understands. "It's me," he cries with a mixture of surprise and childish pleasure. Lange brightens up at once. He tries to point out the artistic qualities of the work. The soccer star nods gravely. Lange's hopes build.

At last the star puts his hand into his pocket. From a distance, the owner of the restaurant follows the proceedings with discernible anxiousness. The soccer star extracts from his pocket a fountain pen, and, with a scrawl like that of a schoolboy, he writes at the bottom of the sketch, "With best wishes, Salomons."

Then he hands the sheet of paper to Lange, gives him a huge, beneficent smile, and goes back to his meal.

XXVIII

A little later in the street Andreina and Moraldo experience their first rift. Hardly had the meal ended when Andreina stood up and announced her wish to go home. Lange gave her a farewell pinch. Gattone who was by then completely drunk tried to kiss her hand again but could hardly get to his feet. Hilda, who had evidently mistaken Andreina for a colleague, gave Andreina her address in the Colosseum area. For a while Andreina walks in silence, without allowing Moraldo to take her arm. He, too, is silent. He feels a profound sense of unhappiness mixed with a muddled feeling of rancor that he is not sure he directs at the others in the restaurant or at himself.

Finally Andreina forces herself to smile. It is an uncertain smile, which does not hide very well her inner turmoil. "It was nice," she says in a low voice. "I like your friends."

Moraldo was expecting something else. This attempt by Andreina to adapt to his former environment touches him.

"No," he states almost brusquely. "I know that you didn't like them. I feel badly about the whole thing."

"Why should you?" Andreina says. Then she adds more faintly, "Those poor people."

For awhile both of them remain silent. Then Andreina takes Moraldo's arm and squeezes it, almost imploring him, with a dark feeling of apprehension. "You aren't like them, are you?" she asks him softly.

"I don't know," Moraldo answers candidly after a moment.

"You don't know?" she says, astonished.

"No," says Moraldo a little bit aggressively. "No one can know exactly who he is or how he is made up. He might be one kind of person today and a different kind tomorrow. No one is consistently the same. If you pigeonhole yourself or other people, you limit life too much. . . . You can't know yourself or other people, not perfectly. . . ."

This kind of an outlook on life is precisely the sort of thing

Andreina's mind rebels against with all its might. For the first time, Moraldo sees what her freshness and charm have hidden up to now, her middle-class mentality. Nevertheless, his feeling for her is still so strong that this aspect arouses tenderness in him instead of alarm.

"Maybe you are right," concludes Moraldo, uncertain and fluctuating in his mind. "Maybe life can be seen clearly. . . ." He becomes more gentle, in order to be forgiven. Deep down inside, Moraldo understands how Andreina must have felt, overwhelmed and offended by those people and their behavior. He takes her arm and asks her to forgive him. It was his fault. He should not have taken her into such a place. But at the same time Moraldo speaks to Andreina, something inside him tells him that he will never be able to be completely sincere with her. There will always be people and things he will have to hide.

Andreina has tears in her eyes. Moraldo dries them with his handkerchief. He covers her face with kisses. The two of them are concealed in the protective shadow of the front door to her building. This evening before they separate, their farewells are prolonged and tender. They want to erase the memory of their rift.

"Tomorrow night, the usual time?" Moraldo asks.

They kiss. Then abruptly Andreina remembers that the next day is Sunday. "But tomorrow is Sunday, sweetheart, and tomorrow you are coming here for dinner," she tells Moraldo.

This is the first Moraldo has heard of any such invitation to Andreina's home. He is puzzled.

"I forgot to tell you," says Andreina. "Mother told me to invite you for tomorrow. She wants to meet you."

"She wants to meet me?" asks Moraldo. He is confused and doesn't know what to reply.

"I have spoken about you so much to her. She knows that when I go out, it is always with you. And also my father would like to meet you. . . . You don't want to come?" In Andreina's voice, there is suddenly a tremor of dismay and reproach.

Moraldo is quick to reassure her. "No, no, darling. I wasn't expecting it. But certainly I will come. What time?"

"At one o'clock. We eat at 1:30. Please be nice. Nicer than you possibly can." Andreina laughs lovingly and gives Moraldo a last kiss and a final caress. Then she runs up the stairs. Before she disappears, she turns and waves to Moraldo.

He listens to the clicking of her high heels on the steps. He is alone. Slowly he walks out into the street and starts back to his apartment. He stops. Then he moves on again. "Engaged? . . . Engaged! Strange, very strange."

XXIX

The next day promptly at one Moraldo arrives at Andreina's home. His state of mind is hard to define. For us to say simply that he is apprehensive would be to say both too little and too much. Rather it is as if he were dreaming. He knows that the visit will be very important, and he experiences it a little bit as would a spectator watching someone else.

Andreina opens the door for him. She gives him a rapid and furtive kiss and squeezes his hand. Andreina leads Moraldo into the small living room, where they are immediately joined by Andreina's younger brother. He is a silent and inquisitive little boy of eight or nine. Immediately Moraldo finds an instinctive sense of comfort in the fact that, through a thousand small details, Andreina's home recalls the home of Moraldo's parents. Each place has about it the same unmistakable air of middle-class orderliness and prosperity.

The mother enters. She is middle-aged and very loquacious. Her constant stream of conversation is perhaps designed to hide her sense of discomfort. Continuously she throws inquiring looks at the young man and at his clothes. Following her mother's glances, Andreina becomes aware that Moraldo's suit is deplorably rumpled, and she begins to feel uneasy. What makes her even more uneasy, though, is that she must play a part in front of her mother. She must not give away the intimate nature of her relationship with Moraldo. It is very clear that the mother has not the slightest suspicion that the two are lovers.

The mother chatters and chatters, and then she offers vermouth in little glasses from a service of six lined up inside a small, glass-fronted cupboard. Moraldo accidentally spills some of his vermouth on his pants.

Loud exclamations come from both women. They seem to have expected this to occur. Andreina proposes immediately that Moraldo take off his pants and let her clean them. The mother approves the plan at once and urges Moraldo to do as Andreina suggests. Moraldo tries feebly to resist, but the two women who are in full accord won't give up.

"Quick, quick, before daddy comes," says Andreina.

"Yes. Don't stand on ceremony," urges the mother. "Andreina is very good at these things."

"Look, you have a stain there. And another one here. . . . In ten minutes, I'll have your pants cleaned and pressed. They're so rumpled anyway."

The two women push Moraldo toward a doorway and make him enter the parents' bedroom. Before closing the double doors, Andreina undoes Moraldo's tie quickly.

"While you're at it, let me have the tie also. I'll give it a quick press," she tells him.

Moraldo takes off his pants and puts them into his future mother-in-law's hand, which protrudes through the double doors. Immediately the hand disappears with the pants. Moraldo is left by himself in his underpants, without his necktie, in the unfamiliar room.

Bewildered, Moraldo looks around him. He walks slowly back and forth. The double bed. The father's bedroom slippers. A forgotten garment on a chair. Photographs of the family in a corner of the room. Exactly the way Moraldo's room will be in a few years. The way his world will be, in a few years. . . .

XXX

The serious conversation begins over coffee. The dinner has been the usual dinner under such circumstances, with comments expected at the end on the success of dessert. Usually the dessert at such dinners is excellent, but this time it could not have been worse if someone had tried to make it worse.

The father, thinks Moraldo, is the most likeable of them all, not counting Andreina, of course. As is the case for all men in such situations, the presence of the suitor for the daughter's hand has placed an unbearable burden on the father. He tries to conceal his discomfort by using elaborately fastidious language, but he does not succeed very well. Now and then, he falters pathetically and slips into slang. Moraldo understands and appreciates the father's predicament. "I'll probably be the same when my turn comes," thinks Moraldo. He sympathizes with this bald man on whom the routine of earning a living has left its mark.

Leaving the dining room, they return to the cramped living room with its terribly uncomfortable chairs. Here they touch on delicate matters. The father inquires about Moraldo's education, the positions he has held in the past, and the work he is doing at present.

Naturally Moraldo lies. He has the impression, however, that the father is well aware Moraldo is lying and only pretends to believe him. The one area in which Moraldo feels he can tell the truth is about his family. Andreina's father recognizes that Moraldo's family is well-to-do and similar to his own. This seems to reassure him.

Meanwhile the radio broadcasts one of its typically atrocious variety shows, sprinkled with jokes by the host and songs sung in falsetto by members of the cast.

"I like that fellow very much," exclaims the mother. "He really makes me laugh. He is so good."

The father pretends that he knows who she is talking about and gravely nods agreement. It is clear, however, that he is completely unable to tell one from another in the cast that so delights his family. The little brother who had been dozing suddenly wakes up and begins to howl. The mother and Andreina scold him.

Trying to ignore the radio and to speak through the bawling of his family, the father says to Moraldo, "If you would like an invitation to that friend of mine. . . . I understand that beginnings are difficult, but if you are willing to work, you can always amount to something. For example, I . . . ." Here he begins the story of his career. He talks about his youth and about the various trials he overcame without batting an eyelash.

Fortunately, Andreina interrupts. She wishes to go to the movies. An excellent film is playing, with an actress she likes very much.

"I'll go too," says the mother, "since father takes his nap now."

"Good idea, mother," exclaims Andreina, genuinely pleased. "Let's go. Get ready."

Heaving a sigh of relief inside himself, the father prepares for his nap. The mother gets ready to go out. Meanwhile Andreina leads Moraldo to her room.

"Do you like my little room?" she asks, a bit excited.

Moraldo feels a bit excited himself. He puts his arms around her and squeezes her. Andreina protests in a choked voice and frees herself.

Outside the bedroom, the radio continues to play and spread its diabolical voice throughout the apartment.

Moraldo thinks to himself, "Is this what life is? Is this the simple secret of life? This quietness? This contentment? This acceptance of certain traditional attitudes and situations?"

XXXI

The incredible always happens. Events come linked together like cherries. The only thing needed to complete the reordering of

Moraldo's life is a job. And one evening, the job that Moraldo sought everywhere since his arrival in the city comes to him as a gift from heaven, when he expects it least.

Returning home from a soup kitchen where he is now reduced to having supper, where at a marble table with a tin spoon he gets a double serving of soup for sixty lire, Moraldo finds in his room an envelope with handwriting on it that he does not recognize. The *commendatore*, that long forgotten man who promised to help Moraldo, has, in fact, found work for him. A position in an office. A large office of a government-run agency with hundreds of employees. Moraldo must undergo a probationary period, but the *commendatore* assures him that with his backing the probationary period will be a mere bureaucratic formality. In short, Moraldo now has a job.

Moraldo takes up the phone and calls Andreina to give her the news. Through the receiver, he listens to her happy exclamations as she relays the news to her family. It dawns on him that his own enthusiasm about the event is considerably less than hers.

"Aren't you pleased?" asks Andreina, puzzled perhaps by the wan quality of his voice.

"Yes, sure. Goddamnit, I'm very pleased," protests Moraldo in spite of himself. It would be a fine thing not to be pleased about such a solution, after all the hunting and waiting. . . .

And so Moraldo gets ready to begin work. This morning, the first day he will go to the office, he feels excited. Andreina has advised him to inspect carefully his clothes, his tie, and his whole appearance. Conscientiously, Moraldo spruces up. He knots his tie as precisely as he can. He brushes his suit meticulously.

Then Moraldo sets out in the street. How beautiful the streets of the city seem to him in the morning. The upward slopes seem to disappear shining into the sky. The old houses with their soft, warm colors. . . . The flower stalls at the bottom of stairways. . . . And especially the people who come and go incessantly with a sense of cheerfulness and a zest for life. . . .

Involuntarily, Moraldo's thoughts turn to that old vagabond Gattone and to that adventurous scoundrel Lange. Moraldo laughs to himself when he thinks of the faces they would make if they knew he was going to become an office worker. But when all is said and done, what has their rebelliousness brought those two? Aren't they both failures?

Moraldo arrives at his destination full of enthusiasm. The main office of the agency is in an enormous palace. The employees are arriving by dozens. Moraldo follows them, but they disperse into a hundred different doors and leave him to find the office of the manager under whose control he will work from now on.

The waiting room of the manager. The waiting. Other employees with folders and sheets of paper enter before Moraldo. With a pang in his heart, Moraldo notes that all of them, especially the older ones, have strange expressions of fear and humility on their faces before they cross the sacred portal.

Finally Moraldo's turn comes. He enters. The manager is a young man, younger than the majority of those Moraldo saw enter with so much apprehension. The manager shows Moraldo an official, if cool, cordiality that, Moraldo thinks, can be attributed only to the letter of recommendation written by the *commendatore*.

An introductory talk on the duties of employees in general and on Moraldo's duties in particular follows. Meanwhile, Moraldo thinks to himself that from now on this man will be the ruler of his days and perhaps of his thoughts.

The manager buzzes his intercom and brings in an elderly employee of the division to which Moraldo is assigned. The manager turns Moraldo over to him.

The two men set out, the elderly employee first, Moraldo a little bit behind him. The corridors are endless. There are doors to the right and to the left, a staircase, more corridors, more doors. . . . Moraldo looks at the slightly bowed back of the man before him.

They enter a room in which two other people are present: an elderly woman with gray hair and a young man approximately twenty-five years old. These two introduce themselves, and after a few moments of polite conversation they go back to their previous activities with a slight air of uncomfortableness over the new-comer's intrusion.

For the time being, Moraldo has no desk of his own. He must be content with sitting cater-cornered at the desk of the young man. In compensation, however, he has nothing special to do. They have told him to help the young man and to learn from him, but the young man himself is doing nothing.

In order to look busy, Moraldo opens two, very thin, green folders on the desk. Inside of each one, there is a copy of a letter and nothing else. The young man explains to Moraldo that the originals have been sent out for signatures. When the originals come back, the young man will mail them.

Moraldo looks around him. The only one working is the old woman. She is copying something from a bound volume. The elderly man seems to be reading and rereading a typewritten sheet of paper. By now he must know it by heart.

"Here I am," thinks Moraldo. "At the top is the manager. Then there is this gray-haired man. Then the young man. And finally me."

He glances at the window. All the visible space outside is blocked by a white wall across a narrow courtyard. Moraldo gets up and goes to the window to try to see beyond the top of the wall. This he barely succeeds in doing by twisting his neck.

"You are lucky to start in this section," says the elderly man who is behind him. "At least this room is nice. I spent ten years down on the ground floor. We had to have the lights on all day."

Moraldo shivers. It's not that the lights had to be kept on which bothers him, but that the poor creature had spent ten years of his life that way and now considers himself lucky because he can spend another ten, or twenty, in this room. "How long have you been here?" Moraldo ventures to ask.

"Here? Seven years. But my desk for the first four was that one. This one belonged to Lorenzetti, the poor fellow." He turns to the old woman. "Do you remember him?"

She nods yes, in silence. Then she explains to Moraldo, "He died two years ago, retired on pension."

The young man is reading a sports paper. "Rome or Lazio?" he asks Moraldo abruptly. When he discovers that Moraldo has no preference between the two soccer teams, he falls back to his reading, profoundly disgusted with Moraldo.

A deathly silence. Far off can be heard the clicking of a typewriter and, every now and then, the ring of a bell.

Slowly the elderly man rises to his feet and makes his way to the coatrack. With nothing else better to do, Moraldo watches his movements. He sees the elderly man search through the pocket of his overcoat, take out a key, return slowly to his desk, open the drawer with his key, take out a handkerchief, and blow his nose.

Fascinated and holding his breath, Moraldo continues to watch. The gray-haired man refolds his handkerchief carefully, replaces it in the drawer, locks the drawer, and carries the key back to the pocket of his overcoat. None of the other two in the room shows any surprise at the elderly man's behavior.

Beads of sweat form on Moraldo's forehead. He feels as if he is suffocating. He springs to his feet. "Can I," he says in a low voice, "can I go out for a few minutes for coffee? This morning, I didn't have time."

The elderly man is perplexed. For some seconds, he does not speak. Perhaps he is weighing the pros and cons of this unheard-of request. The mysterious letter of recommendation that Moraldo has behind him is the decisive factor. All right, go ahead. It's the first morning. . . . But hurry up, for heaven's sake. He doesn't want the responsibility.

Moraldo grabs his overcoat and bolts through the door. He scrambles down the stairs, crosses the cold marble entryway, and runs out into the street.

In the street he rediscovers the sun, the strolling people, the flower stalls, and the upward slopes that disappear in the sky. He walks rapidly, without looking back, as if fleeing a mortal danger.

XXXII

For that evening Moraldo has arranged a meeting with Andreina, who is anxious to learn how things went during her fiancé's first day in the office.

Throughout the day Moraldo has stayed out of sight and has avoided social contacts. His state of mind as he goes to the meeting is not clear even to him.

Going along the street, Moraldo encounters Ricci standing in the doorway of a bar. Ricci stops Moraldo with his customary gesture of mocking and paternal curiosity. "What are you up to?" he asks Moraldo.

They haven't seen each other for a long time. Ricci has been in the provinces.

"A job. . . . I'm engaged," says Moraldo.

Ricci congratulates him but also looks Moraldo up and down with the customarily sly expression on his face, which indicates that Ricci believes only half of what he hears. "Come see me," he urges Moraldo. "But don't telephone the apartment. I'm never there." He winks at Moraldo with some implication Moraldo can't fathom. "I'm here." Ricci points to a corner of the bar Ciao.

Then Ricci draws Moraldo aside. "If your fiancée needs any linens. . . ." Ricci sees from Moraldo's face that it would be useless to go on. He waves good-by and looks off in a different direction placidly.

Moraldo arrives at the meeting spot a little late. Andreina has been waiting for him in front of a furniture dealer's store. She comes toward him with gaiety and curiosity.

"How did it go? Come on, tell me all about it. What things did they have you do? Were you clever?"

Moraldo doesn't answer at once. Perhaps he is on the verge of giving her a truthful answer, but something holds him back, as if he realizes one piece of the truth will lead to more. "Well, the first day, you know how it is. There's not much to do. . . . It was sort of boring," he tells her.

"It's better if you don't have too much work," she observes. "Certainly, at first, when you aren't used to the office, everything seems hard. But later on . . . you'll see."

She takes his arm and gives him a squeeze to comfort him. She chuckles at the expression on his face, which is unenthusiastic. "So the little man had trouble getting used to things, did he? . . . But now it's time to become sensible. Now there's Andreina to think of, and a home, and a family," she says in a joking tone. She gives Moraldo a little kiss. Then she turns Moraldo toward the store's window display and points out to him the bed frames, the highly polished chests of drawers, and the easy-chairs without slipcovers.

Andreina gets excited. Wouldn't a room like that be wonderful? But with a less exotic fabric. That one would get on her nerves after a while. Would she like something in bright pink? Yes, she would very much. For the dining room, though. . . .

While Andreina goes on talking, Moraldo remains silent. However, he feels words rising irresistibly from his heart to his lips. These are words he has refused to speak up until now. But the words are coming nearer and nearer to his lips.

"Listen, Andreina," he says suddenly, as if someone else were speaking in his place. "That job. I quit it. I walked out this morning, and I didn't go back. I'm not going to go back ever again!"

Andreina breaks off. Dismayed and very alarmed, she stares at him. "Why?"

In the face of her dismay, Moraldo feels himself soften. But perhaps it is this very feeling that drives him on to be totally sincere once and for all with her and also with himself. Everything that he refused to acknowledge inside him now comes out.

"I can't marry you, Andreina. I would make you unhappy. We would not be happy together. I really believed that I could adapt to that kind of life: you, the job, the home. . . . But I realize now that it isn't true. I can't do it. I don't know what I want or what I'll end up doing, but now I'm sure of what I don't want.

That way of life. . . . You must forgive me, Andreina. I really do love you. I feel terrible saying these things to you, but it is better for both of us."

Andreina is white as a sheet. Her lips quiver. She seems lost and frightened. "Are you in love with someone else?" she asks, with her feminine logic.

"No, no, I swear it," says Moraldo. "The thought of not seeing you any more, of losing you, makes me suffer very much. I swear it. If that weren't true, I would have spoken back at the start. It's just that. . . ." Again, distressed and tender at the same time, Moraldo tries to explain to the girl those things that aren't completely clear even to himself.

Andreina understands only partially. What she does know is that Moraldo will not marry her and that he wants to leave her. This knowledge makes her shiver and cry.

A dozen times, Moraldo comes to the verge of denying everything he has said, of drawing Andreina into his arms, and of promising to start over again with her. But always an insistent voice ringing out inside him warns him against such a mistake, and he stands firm. And so Moraldo's relationship with Andreina comes to an end. He loses her. A road he might have followed is sealed off to him, a road promising serene, peaceful, and sweet things.

Moraldo watches the girl move away among the people and disappear. A profound agony rips at his heart. For the last time he is seized with the temptation to run after his fiancée. But he remains firm. Then suddenly, without his willing it, the anguish inside him becomes transformed into an irrational sense of joy. It is a joy that Moraldo is ashamed of, but a joy that pulls him along with a light step. It is a joy such as he has not felt for a long time, not since he had begun the relationship with Andreina.

Free. Free again. To do what? He doesn't know, but that isn't important to him right now. He walks away, almost skipping, through the evening city, in the flow of pedestrians, without turning to look behind him.

XXXIII

"Do you know what happened? They took Gattone to the hospital!" The voice of Lange echoes in the telephone receiver with an urgency that Moraldo has not heard before.

"To the hospital? Why?" asks Moraldo.

"I don't know much. I was told about it by one of the people at the movie studio where Gattone was working. He was an extra. This person said that they found him in the street unable to stay on his feet with a fever. They had to carry him to the hospital. He didn't want to go. It must be his old problem, his liver."

"Let's go see him right away. Where is he?"

"At Isola Tiberina. I'll meet you there in half an hour."

Moraldo hangs up the receiver and rushes out of his room.

Half an hour later, with Lange, he enters the hall of the ancient building on the island in the Tiber. Both of the men are upset and worried. They go into the main office.

"Gattone? Ah, yes. . . . Ward three on the third floor."

The two men climb enormous, baroque, marble stairs that reek of disinfectant. They pass interns carelessly dressed in jackets that are more gray than white. Through glass doors, they see very long wards, as vast as churches, with many beds lined up. When they reach the third floor, they stop and look around. Both men have become paler.

"Ward three, please?"

The intern indicates a large glass door through which they see a kind of huge, baroque room dominated at the far end by a gigantic canopy in marble supported against the wall by two angels also in marble. The canopy is enough to give anyone the shivers. It seems an entryway to death.

Moraldo and Lange enter the ward cautiously, holding their breath. Slowly they go forward and look at the faces of the people in the lines of white beds to the left and to the right.

When they are halfway through the ward, they hear a hoarse voice coming from the far end, almost from the area beneath the huge canopy. The voice cries out, rolling its r's: "Craven cowards! Release me! I want to leave. Cowards!"

The voice of Gattone? Moraldo and Lange look at each other and hurry forward.

In the last bed they see Gattone. His face is purple. His eyes are glazed with delirium. Gattone tosses on his bed and continues shouting with all the force he can muster. "Get me out of here. I don't want to die here. Release me!"

Suddenly Gattone sees the two friends who stand speechless several feet away. In spite of his delirium, he recognizes them. "Moraldo! Lange! Come here!" he rasps in a lower voice. "Come here, Moraldo!"

White as a ghost, Moraldo steps closer.

"They have me fastened in with barbed wire," continues Gattone in his rasping voice. "Release me! Put me on my feet! I want to get out of here!"

Moraldo looks around as if seeking help. Someone in a nearby bed says, "He's been shouting since this morning. He tries to roll out of the bed."

Moraldo moves closer still. Pity has overcome fear. He puts his hand on Gattone's arm. "Don't shout. Calm down. We'll get the doctor now."

Gattone, however, won't listen to reason. He succeeds in throwing back the covers. In his hospital gown he looks like a little baby. His legs which have traveled the world are white and puny. They seem the thin legs of an old man. Two loose bands of cloth hold the legs fastened to the bed.

An intern comes into the ward. He brushes past Moraldo, puts the covers back over Gattone, and resettles Gattone in the bed.

Gattone cries out and tosses.

"What's wrong with him? Why is he like this?" exclaims the frightened Moraldo.

"Please move away," says the intern a little dryly. "He's worse when he sees people. . . . He's delirious." Then the intern pushes them back. Lange is so frightened that he can hardly breathe. He doesn't need to be urged much to move away. Moraldo, however, delays.

"What does he have? What are you doing for him?" he asks.

The intern shrugs. "Cirrhosis of the liver. He's toxic. Because of this, he is in a state of delirium. The kidneys aren't functioning. . . . We'll see tomorrow. . . ."

"Can he be cured?" insists Moraldo.

Again the intern shrugs.

In silence Moraldo and Lange walk out into the little square in front of the hospital. They haven't the strength to discuss the situation. They agree to come back in the early evening.

XXXIV

When Moraldo and Lange return, they go up at once to the vast ward dominated by the marble angels. This time, however, the voice of Gattone is not to be heard. At first the two men do not grasp the significance of the silence. Then they find themselves before Gattone's bed. It is empty. The mattress is rolled back. They look at each other in silence.

"Are you friends of Gattone?" asks someone behind them. His voice is one they have not heard before. It is a courteous voice with an obviously foreign accent. The speaker, however, rolls his r's in the same manner as Gattone did.

They turn and find standing before them a little man in his forties. He wears a dirty, beat-up raincoat similar to the one Gattone wore. He introduces himself. His name is French. Neither Moraldo nor Lange has ever heard of him.

"He died two hours ago," explains this man in a low voice. "They took the body downstairs."

There is a pause. The three men walk together in silence toward the door.

"I've been to the office," resumes the little man. "They gave me Gattone's watch and his billfold to send to his daughter."

"Gattone has a daughter?" asks Lange surprised.

"Yes, a married daughter in Norway."

"And you? Excuse me for asking, but who are you?" says Lange with his customary frankness.

"I've known Gattone for many years. I'm a writer too. We worked together in Paris in '35."

Moraldo and Lange embrace and shake hands with this mysterious new Gattone, who seems to have been created expressly to continue the heritage of Gattone. The two friends leave together.

Later, as Moraldo returns to his room alone, he feels exhausted. He realizes that his own death could resemble what he has witnessed. Like Gattone, Moraldo has refused, and continues to refuse, all those things that are normal and regular. But what is it he is aiming for? What is he looking for?

Although it is late, Moraldo's landlady is still up. A little worried, she comes to meet him. She whispers mysteriously, "There's a man here waiting for you."

Moraldo becomes cross. "A man? Who is he?"

"I don't know. He was here earlier today looking for you, and then two hours ago he came back."

Moraldo experiences a sudden foreboding. Cautiously he opens the door to his room and enters.

Stretched out on the bed, fully dressed, is Moraldo's father. Evidently during the long wait he fell asleep.

Moraldo's heart contracts in anguish. His father came looking for him on this night of all nights. . . . "Papa," calls Moraldo softly.

The father wakes up with a start. For a moment, he finds it hard to get his bearings. He gives his son an embarrassed smile. Then he gets up from the bed and embraces Moraldo. The son allows himself to be embraced. Both of them feel uneasy.

"I had to come to the city to get some things straightened out at the Ministry. I looked for you at the old address. You weren't there any more. . . ."

"Yes, I moved a little while ago," Moraldo explains evasively.

"How is mama?" he asks his father. "And Sandra?"

The father gives him the news from home. The mother has her usual ailments a little more frequently, but in general she is well. Sandra expects another baby.

"Another baby?" The news, for some reason, affects Moraldo strangely. But, of course, on this night everything affects him in a special way.

"And you? What are you doing?" asks the father. The father glances quickly, but expressively, at the shabby room, the worn-out clothes, and the tormented face of his son. The glance is filled with a silent anxiety.

For an instant, Moraldo is on the verge of telling his father the whole truth about his existence. He is on the verge of surrendering. But then he lies: "Things are good. I found a job. Right now I'm in the probationary period, but soon. . . ."

The father is quiet for a few moments. Then, uneasily, he hazards, "Your mother wonders if you wouldn't like to come home for a while, maybe a few months. We could find you a job there, too. . . ."

Moraldo smiles. It is a stiff, forced smile. "No. Thank you. I can't give up this job, you see . . . now that I've found it."

The father understands. He doesn't insist. His face says clearly for him what he thinks and how much sadness he feels.

Here for the last time an opportunity for firm mooring, for a safe haven, has been offered to Moraldo, at a moment when he is perhaps the most disconsolate in his life. And Moraldo has refused it.

The following morning the father departs.

XXXV

That evening Lange reappears. He is again the usual devil-may-care Lange. The tragic event of the preceding day seems to have slipped from his mind without leaving a trace.

"Do you have a girl friend you can get hold of easily?" he asks

Moraldo bluntly. "No? Ah, well, it doesn't really matter. I'll dig up the women myself. . . . Tomorrow night, come to my studio. We'll have a party. An orgy!"

Moraldo has trouble understanding. For a moment, he thinks Lange is joking. But Lange, who is already walking off in his eccentric, loose-jointed way, calls back, "Around nine. My place. Bring some wine."

At nine the following evening, Moraldo climbs the long, dark, narrow steps to Lange's studio. He has under his arm a fiasco of wine that he has bought with money left him by his father. Up to the last moment, Moraldo had been unsure he would come. The death of Gattone and the visit of his father had troubled Moraldo profoundly. Then, perhaps out of instinct, alone, in a desperate state, he set out for Lange's studio.

The studio is on the top floor of an old, foul-smelling building. When Moraldo arrives there, he finds Lange very busy trying to get his grubby milieu in better order.

With Lange is a girl whom Moraldo has never seen before. She is neither pretty nor ugly. She could be a salesgirl in a store, or she could be a maid. She bustles about helping Lange and seems to enjoy the excitement of preparing for a party.

"Put it there. Put it there," Lange tells Moraldo, indicating a portion of the room hidden behind a screen. Moraldo goes in back of the screen and discovers a small, unmade bed, a dripping sink, a partially broken chair, and here and there on the floor bottles and plates of food. Moraldo puts his bottle with the others.

Meanwhile Lange continues talking in a loud voice on the other side of the screen. "Did you ever see so much stuff? It was all bought by an engineer named Ansaldi. I am painting his villa in Frascati. He has been after me for quite a while. . . . He wants to enjoy himself among the 'artists.'" Lange guffaws.

"For him, it's as if Gattone never existed," thinks Moraldo to himself, "or else died twenty years ago."

Then the other guests arrive. There is a shabbily dressed girl with straight, shoulder-length hair hanging along her gaunt cheeks: a late-blooming existentialist. Another girl who is large, jolly, awkward, and as brash as an overgrown puppy. A very small and aggressive man who is a friend of Lange. And finally, there is the Maecenas, the engineer from Frascati, who is in his forties, stout, and very properly dressed. The engineer dries his stubby, sweaty little hands continually and looks around the studio with an uneasy smile full of the illicit hopes men usually experience in whorehouses.

The studio is small, and the guests are squeezed together. No one knows where to sit. Every now and then, someone bumps into a stand with wet, sticky clay on it. Lange and the girl who is helping him become nervous. Then there is a knock at the door.

Lange is surprised. He doesn't expect anyone else. The engineer blushes. He explains that he took the liberty of inviting a woman he knows. She is a writer and an intellectual.

"Excellent. Let the writer in!" cries Lange.

Someone opens the door, and there on the threshold stands Signora Contini. She is accompanied by a young man, roughly Moraldo's age, but blond instead of brown-haired.

At first she does not see Moraldo among all the people. He, of course, sees her and stays back, full of uneasiness. Then by force of circumstances, they come together face to face. For a moment, the woman, too, experiences a sense of sharp discomfort, but quickly she overcomes it with her habitual pose of easy superiority. She offers her hand to Moraldo and says to him with seeming spontaneity, "Oh! How are you? It's been some time now since I've seen you. . . . May I introduce . . . ?" She presents the latest gigolo. Moraldo shakes hands with his alter ego and then immediately jerks back his hand in disgust.

Elsewhere in the room the people have found seats as best they could. They are feigning animated conversation, but in reality they feel ill at ease. The short journalist pours the first glass of wine. Lange appears with a plate of cold meats as the antipasto course.

Signora Contini pretends to look around as if she were

gathering material. "It's interesting," she says to someone nearby. "I adore this turn-of-the-century Bohemian tone." She drinks her wine slowly and glances at Moraldo, whom she has not spoken to since her arrival.

With the excuse of checking on the pasta, one of the men goes behind the screen where some of the girls are. The first words of protest can be heard clearly by all in the studio. "What do you think you're doing? Let's not start, eh? . . . Keep your hands off me!"

The engineer continues to look around with eyes shining, waiting for scandalous events to occur. For the moment, however, there is only the painful, false animation. The sole hope lies in the wine, and Lange is pouring it out unstintingly.

Hours later, the atmosphere has changed. In a small space cleared among the chairs, the existentialist girl is dancing the samba with her eyes staring off into space and hair over her face. Around her swirl confused shouts and ear-shattering shrieks of laughter.

Almost everyone is drunk. But it is a flat, dull drunkenness without inventiveness or pleasure. All inhibitions have fallen away. Yet everything is, nevertheless, still painful and squalid. The girls protest against advances one minute and then pour out aggressive phrases of love the next.

Moraldo is the only one not drunk. He is very white. It seems to him he is awake in the midst of a nightmare. He is unable to take his eyes away from his former lover in whom he witnesses a tragic transformation.

The mask of elegant, intellectual haughtiness has fallen from the face of Signora Contini. The animal impulses in her have been released. She embraces her blond young man fiercely and kisses him without inhibition. Then she stretches her arm toward Moraldo and calls him, "Come on. Come over here. Let's make up. . . . Don't be jealous. Come here and give me a little kiss." And she laughs raucously.

Lange has already fallen asleep, his head tilted back in his chair. . . .

Later as the first white light of morning enters through the dirty window, Moraldo wakes up. Around him are the awkwardly stretched out bodies of wheezing sleepers. In the cemeterial light, amid clay figures and shreds of paper, the sleepers seem to be cadavers.

It's cold. Moraldo shivers. He sits up and looks around him. He is frightened and exhausted. Another shiver runs through him. It is a stronger one. His whole body shakes.

Moraldo gets to his feet slowly. He straightens out his clothes. He tiptoes carefully across the room, trying not to step on anyone, and goes out onto the landing. In the foul-smelling darkness he stops near a faucet set in the wall and splashes water on his face.

XXXVI

The streets are still semideserted and gray. Moraldo walks randomly through them, his collar turned up, his hands in his pockets, and his head down.

Moraldo is in a depression that deepens with every step. It is as if all the delusions accumulated in these months of struggles and experiences had gushed forth from a deep spring at the bottom of his consciousness.

He doesn't know anything. He doesn't understand anything. He has the impression that he will never succeed in understanding anything about life or about people.

A trolley that runs to the outskirts of town stops a few feet away from Moraldo. Without thinking, Moraldo boards the trolley.

The trolley is full of workmen. At each stop more get on. Their faces are hardened by a fatigue that nocturnal sleep does not dispel. Their clothes are dirty, and their hands heavy. These human beings are sad, burdened, and without light. At least that is the way Moraldo sees them. Their faces, which rise up in waves and crowd around him, terrify him and give him the feeling of being by himself among unknown and hostile creatures.

Moraldo's anguish is so intense that he has trouble breathing. Moments such as these are the moments when thoughts of suicide ripen. Suicide may seem the only possible solution.

At the extreme edge of the city, Moraldo leaves the trolley and walks slowly into the countryside. Troubling questions assail him. "What am I looking for? What am I? A little bit venal, but not too much. I wasn't able to adapt like that blond gigolo. . . . A little bit middle class, but not too much. I threw away Andreina, the job, and my home. . . . Gattone? To be like Gattone? To die like him? Just to think of that terrifies me. . . . Well, then, what is it I'm looking for? What is it I want?"

Moraldo leaves the road. He sits down on the grass. Then as if conquered by the unendurable weight of the darkness enfolding him, he stretches out prone and lies still.

XXXVII

That evening, when the first lights come on in the line of dark houses of the city, Moraldo awakens. A kind of heavy torpor has held him throughout the entire day.

Without knowing how, Moraldo finds his way to the broad highway studded with lights leading back into the center of the city. He looks down the highway at the houses and at the human movement. The buzz of the people carries to him. He does not go forward. Something seems to pull him back toward the countryside, which is veiled in darkness. He is afraid. He has no wish to plunge back into the midst of things, no wish at all to begin again.

A car brakes loudly to a halt a few feet away. Moraldo turns toward the car slowly as if in a dream.

"What are you doing?" Protruding through the window of the battered, little black Fiat is the mocking, foxlike face of Ricci. "Come on. Get in. I'll give you a lift. What are you doing out here?" With the motor still running, Ricci opens a door.

Moraldo walks slowly toward the car. He hesitates a moment and then shakes his head. "No. Thank you."

"You won't come with me? . . . Do you have a girl stashed away out here?" Ricci asks. Then he notices something unusual in Moraldo's face. "What has happened?" he says. Moraldo shrugs. There is a lump in his throat. He finds it difficult to speak.

"No money, huh? That's not so bad." Ricci fumbles in his pockets. "Will five hundred lire be enough until tomorrow?"

Moraldo smiles slightly and pushes back the money. "No, that isn't the problem."

"Then what is the problem? You have money in your pockets. You're young. What else could you want?" asks the astonished Ricci.

"I've had enough," says Moraldo in a hoarse voice.

"Enough of what?"

"Of everything."

There is silence. Ricci turns off the motor and gets out of the car. He has become serious. His seriousness is a little comic, but it is sincere. He takes out a partially crumpled pack of cigarettes. He offers Moraldo a cigarette and puts one in his own mouth. Ricci would like to say something helpful, but he can't think what to say. Then suddenly, he blurts out, "Ah, Goddamnit! It's a good thing you didn't accept."

Moraldo doesn't understand.

"The five hundred lire. . . . Tomorrow a note falls due. I wasn't thinking."

Another brief silence, and then Ricci continues. "Do you know they want to declare me bankrupt? Goddamnit all! Two warrants. My life is hell. I can't go home. And my wife knows nothing about all this."

He explains confidentially, "I happened to sign my wife's name on the notes . . . to get around the bankruptcy proceedings." He pauses a moment. "The poor woman. Every now and then, I tell her a tall tale, just to pump a little hope into her. Yesterday I told her I was putting together a deal worth two million lire. A question of a few days." He laughs, delighted by his own story.

Then, brusquely, Ricci asks Moraldo, "But what is going on with you? What kind of job do you have?"

Moraldo shrugs his shoulders. "Nothing. I don't know how to do anything . . . either well or badly." Then, more softly, he adds with a stiff smile, "What's the use in continuing?"

Ricci remains pensive for several moments, muttering to himself. Then suddenly, very seriously, as if he had hit upon a brilliant solution, he asks, "Have you ever tried the automobile business?"

Surprised, Moraldo stares at Ricci. At first he believes that Ricci is joking. But Ricci is perfectly serious. Ricci has interpreted Moraldo's drama in terms of Ricci's own outlook on life and has found a solution in accord with that outlook.

Ricci warms to his subject. "I have a friend who has made big money selling cars. I'll introduce you. It's not my kind of enterprise, but you are young, and you have a distinguished appearance. . . ."

For a while, Ricci goes on explaining animatedly the advantages and possibilities of his solution. The disheartened Moraldo listens to him without showing any reaction. But, instead of frightening Moraldo, the stubborn and incomprehensible vitality of Ricci gradually disarms him.

Moraldo lets Ricci finish and then asks him point-blank, "But you? Don't you ever get tired? Don't you ever have enough of all this struggling?"

A little surprised, Ricci looks at him. He waves his hand up and down, the fingers together out straight. "Good grief, you've got to stay alive."

Life in spite of everything. The mass of darkness lodged in Moraldo's heart begins to crumble into pieces.

Again Ricci insists, "Come on. Get in the car. I'll take you back to the city."

Moraldo refuses again. No, really no. He needs to be alone for a while longer.

Ricci gets back into the car and starts the motor. "Tomorrow come to the bar. . . . No, the day after tomorrow. Tomorrow I can't make it. . . . I'll introduce you to that person in car sales. . . . Listen, as a favor, though, if you telephone the house, don't let anything slip to my wife. Even if she asks. Keep things quiet." With a final wave and a final wink, Ricci drives off.

Moraldo is alone. He watches the battered, little black Fiat move away and rattle down the street. Now Moraldo advances toward the city, slowly at first, and then with a quicker step. An irrational exuberance comes over him little by little.

The lights around him now seem gay. And the faces, the faces of the crowd that walks alongside him, they now seem less hostile. A brunette girl walks by him with her opulent hair bouncing in waves on her shoulders. She gives Moraldo a flashing smile.

Farther on, a boy in shirtsleeves rides his bicycle past Moraldo. The boy whistles a song. . . . Two young lovers come toward him. They hold tightly to each other as they walk. . . . A baby cries. Voices of women intermingle. . . . Life, life, with its inexhaustible, unforeseeable treasure of encounters, chance events, people, and adventures.

Moraldo walks briskly among the people, smiling at everybody.

Moraldo as played by Franco Interlenghi in *I Vitelloni,* the film to which *Moraldo in the City* was to be a sequel.

The young Fellini as portrayed by Peter Gonzales on his first day in the city in *Roma*. This autobiographical protagonist resembles Moraldo in that he attempts to test himself in the city and achieve the independence of an adult.

The ending of *Nights of Cabiria*, which seems to be a reworking of the final scene in *Moraldo in the City*. The downcast Cabiria has her spirits raised by a festive group of passersby, as Moraldo has his raised by the people around him while he walks back toward the center of the city.

The uninhibited dance of Sylvia (Anita Ekberg) in the nightclub of the Baths of Caracalla in *La Dolce Vita*, which resembles closely the energetic and sexual dance Anita performs at the farmhouse in *A Journey with Anita*.

The young protagonist of *Amarcord* attempting a sexual overture toward Gradisca, the town vamp. The scene was written earlier as one of the memories of Guido in *A Journey with Anita*.

The terrace of the Grand Hotel in *Amarcord*. The scene seems to be a version of Guido's memory of a restaurant by the sea, a spot of glittering sophistication, in *A Journey with Anita*.

The funeral cortege in *Amarcord*. Like the procession in *A Journey with Anita*, the cortege moves through town to the cemetery in inappropriately splendid weather.

The ending of *La Dolce Vita*, where Paola, a young girl from Umbria, smiles sadly and waves good-by to the hero, as Anita does to Guido at the end of *A Journey with Anita*. In both cases , the women seem images of a simple and attractive life left behind by heroes who return to the city.

A Journey with Anita

By Federico Fellini
With Tullio Pinelli

I

In an ancient palace in the middle of Rome, during a sultry afternoon in the summer, a publishing house has organized a literary reception for a famous Chinese writer.

The Chinese writer ends a toast. With a mysterious smile, he responds to the applause of those around him by clapping delicately with his own small, yellow hands.

After the excitement of the toasting has died down, a dull buzz of conversation resumes in the grand hall of the cardinal. The presence of a foreign colleague who speaks only his incomprehensible native language causes a feeling of uneasiness among the Italian guests. Even the most zealous fail to make contact with him. Some who wish to help out the host editor ask the Chinese writer to autograph copies of his translated novel. Then, however, they can only puzzle over the indecipherable flourishes they have obtained.

Guido is seated in the back of the room on a seventeenth-century chair of carved wood. He is bored. Near him an elderly novelist is lobbying for support of his candidacy in the next union elections, and a younger, more irreverent writer jokes about Italian-Chinese relations. The buzzing of cliché expressions, the excessive baroque richness of the patrician salon, and the smiling, inscrutable Asian face combine to transform Guido's boredom gradually into annoyance and malaise. When a young novelist with a bull neck and thick mat of hair begins to regale the host in an Apulian accent[1] with a discourse on the social achievements of Communist countries, Guido gets up and slips out without attracting attention.

This translation is based on a typed manuscript in the possession of Fellini's literary executor, Daniel Keel, Diogenes Verlag, Zurich. It is dated July 1957.

[1] Apulian is the southern accent of the province of Puglia, which is located in the heel of the boot of Italy. To a northerner, such as Guido, the accent would probably be comic. The discourse of the young novelist obviously strikes Guido as stereotypical of a young intellectual.

II

Guido is a fully mature man in his late thirties. A sanguine, self-confident, irreverent, and amusing fellow, he has the look of an intellectual who is successful and well known. There is nothing fatuous about him, however. He has enough common sense to avoid fatuousness and self-satisfaction. He has also a fervid imagination and can pass easily from amusement to boredom or from zestfulness to melancholy. Such rapid shifting, in fact, constitutes the basic law of his personality. If his melancholic periods spring from anything more profound and mysterious, or if his various tremors reflect anything more deep, than the passing crises of an anguishing intellectual, Guido has never been able to discover what these profounder causes are.

Today Guido is in a period of boredom and melancholy. The uneasiness that took possession of him when he was contemplating the unfathomable little eyes of the Chinese writer has not left him, but has even increased now that he has returned home. The moment strikes him as strange. His wife Gianna is out shopping, and the domestic helper is nowhere to be seen.

In the brand new apartment everything shows that the inhabitants have just moved in. It appears that work has just been finished or perhaps not quite finished. The brightness of the colors and of the furnishings makes the apartment seem suspended in a provisional state. It does not have a lived-in feel to it yet.

The empty bedroom with its neatly made double bed, the huge, bright easy chairs standing unoccupied in the living room with its glass doors, and the silence of the deserted rooms made heavier by the invisible presence of the domestic helper moving about in the kitchen add to Guido's feeling of uneasiness. He walks from room to room almost as if he were seeing them for the first time. He sits down, then changes chairs, picks up a book, exchanges it for another, and finally gets to his feet again.

Suddenly the telephone rings. It has the long penetrating ring of a long-distance call, and it startles him.

Someone is calling from Fano. In the few moments that elapse between the words of the operator and the beginning of the conversation with the caller, rapid thoughts race through Guido's mind. Fano is the town on the Adriatic coast where Guido was born. His family lives there still. His father, his mother, his sister. . . . Someone is coming to Rome? . . . Someone is ill? . . . How long since he heard from them? . . . Eight months? . . . A year? . . .

"Hello . . . Guido . . . this is Gina. . . .[2] Can you hear me?"

It is his sister. Her distant voice fades away, returns in a loud blare for a few seconds, and then fades away. Other faint voices come on the line, and then they, too, fade away.

"Hello . . . Guido. . . . Papa is ill. . . . Please come immediately. . . ."

Was that really what she said? Guido isn't sure he has heard correctly. Perhaps he does not want to believe he even received this unexpected telephone call.

"Operator, I can't hear. . . . Hello . . . Gina. . . . Can you hear me? . . . What did you say before? . . . What has happened to papa? . . ."

The voice of his sister is garbled.

"I must come? . . . But is it serious? . . . What has happened to him? . . ."

In Guido's voice, there is more annoyance and incredulity than anxiety. The answer he gets is again garbled.

"It would be a good thing . . . if you can. . . . He had. . . ."

Guido is not able to make out what his father had, but he has the impression that it was something he has gotten over and not something to be deeply alarmed about. At any rate, Guido shouts into the telephone as the conversation is about to end, "Okay, okay. . . . I'll try to come. . . .I'll do what I can. . . . Give my love to mama."

---

[2] Fellini gives the name of the sister here as Anna. Later in the typescript, he gives it as Gina. I have used the name Gina throughout on the supposition that it represents his final choice.

III

Silence fills the apartment again. Pensive and agitated, Guido sits back in an easy chair. He is not sure what is going on inside him. The sudden recall of thoughts about his parents has disconcerted him. It has been many years since he left his home and his family. Only rarely has he returned. Each visit was hurried, and each left him with a sense of definite separation with neither party able to understand the other. Now his father is ill? . . . What does that phrase mean? . . . That he is on the verge of dying perhaps?

The noise of the front door being opened and the sound of his wife's footsteps in the hallway attract his attention. However, Guido does not move. He stays in his chair, wrapped in silence, without any outward sign of life. Certainly Gianna does not expect him to be home at this hour of the day, and Guido wants to see what she does when she comes home. This is not the love game of an enamored husband, however. It is the tactic of a bored mate to put off the moment of reengagement with familial life— to hang back from it for a few minutes.

Gianna is slender and elegant. She has straight, shiny black hair that falls on her shoulders. When suddenly she discovers her husband before her, her first reaction is one of suspicion rather than surprise. In her refinement she masks her suspicion almost at once, but Guido notices it nevertheless. After seven years of marriage, this concealed suspiciousness of Gianna has become a continuing part of their relationship. Young still and without children, they live together in a conventionally formal way. Their love has become tired.

Not until the evening meal does Guido tell his wife about the telephone call from Fano. Perhaps he speaks of it more out of a desire to break the silence than out of necessity. The table is arranged in the coldly affected manner depicted in illustrated magazines. Gianna, who comes from an upper-middle-class background, holds strongly to such things as white gloves for the woman who serves the meal and finger bowls at the end of the dinner. Her increasing distance from Guido, in whom she used to love the man of letters, has brought into the foreground the fashionable façade of her life with women friends, canasta games, and cocktail parties, and it has driven away all that there was in her, or could have been in her, of more lively interests.

Guido speaks of his father and of his father's illness offhandedly. He doesn't believe that his father is seriously ill. It doesn't seem to Guido that he needs to go to his father, at least not now. Guido has many things to do, many obligations. . . . Tomorrow he will send a telegram asking for clarification, and then he will see. . . . Guido's tone becomes a little too casual and bemused as he recalls the long periods of time devoted to digesting meals by his father, the convivial, hearty eater, which Guido used to witness when he was a boy, and Gianna, instead of being amused, feels offended by Guido's tone.

The coldness of her reaction makes them fall silent again. This silence continues until they go to bed. The prospect of the intimacy of a night together in the bed increases the unexpected tension, the emptiness that has grown between them.

Gianna falls asleep at once. Guido does not. He hears the hours ticking away and listens as the street noises diminish and disappear. Guido lies with his eyes open in the darkness, wide awake. He looks at the sleeping Gianna. A feeling of tenderness, which is a little detached, but still sincere, possesses him suddenly. There come to his mind images of Gianna as she was when they married: a young girl with a face still childlike, not the face of the grand lady of today. Very softly in order not to wake her, Guido grazes his fingers over her face in a caress.

Quietly Guido slips out of bed and leaves the room. Gianna has heard nothing. She sleeps on. Guido tiptoes from room to room, pausing every now and then before moving again. In the silence of the night the furniture and the objects take on a different appearance. The rooms seem strange somehow—perhaps larger or smaller than before. In the kitchen the gleaming, new

lacquered appliances have something menacing about them.
Guido opens the refrigerator, looks through it, gets a drink of ice
water, and moves on.

From a dark corner, the cat emerges noiselessly. He comes
toward Guido on silent paws, with his large green eyes blinking,
a little surprised by this intrusion into his mysterious night life.
The cat follows Guido silently into the living room, jumps onto an
easy chair with a soft purr, and sits staring at Guido with cold
curiosity.

Taking a seat also, Guido lights a cigarette and then puts it
out almost immediately. He goes to close the glass doors, being
careful not to make noise. Guido walks over to the telephone,
picks up the receiver, and then puts it back again. He is worried
and uncertain. The cat remains in his chair, watching like a small
sphinx. Guido picks up the receiver once again and this time dials
a number quickly while keeping an eye on the doors. The ringing
at the other end of the line echoes so loudly in the receiver that it
seems to invade all corners of Guido's silent home. No one
answers. Five, six times, the telephone rings. Yet at the other end,
no one hears it.

Guido's face shows his irritation and uncertainty. He hangs
up the telephone, sits down next to the cat, strokes him distract-
edly, and speaks to him in a whisper. The cat listens in an impas-
sive, dignified manner as if he were a true nocturnal confidant.
Guido continues talking; this game of confiding his anxiety to the
cat amuses him, or at least distracts him, for a few moments.

Leaving the cat, Guido walks to the window. He parts the
full curtains of white muslin and opens the window. In the distance below, a whitish streak of light announces the coming of
day.

Suddenly Guido arrives at a decision. In fact, he is seized
with a frenzy to act immediately. In the hall there is a large
armoire. Guido opens it, pulls out a suitcase, reenters the bedroom quickly without trying to be quiet anymore, and turns on
the light. Gianna wakes up with a start and then sleepily watches

him move rapidly about the room, opening drawers, taking out clothes, and throwing them into the suitcase.

"I'm going to see how Papa is," Guido tells her. "I'm a little worried. . . . I thought it would be the best thing. . . . As soon as I get there, I'll send a telegram, but you'll see that I'll be back here again by Thursday. . . ."

Guido is now in the process of getting dressed. Gianna has lain back down again. "Do you want me to help you?" she asks sleepily.

Hurriedly Guido says no. We might suspect from his tone that he wants to get away before Gianna can offer to accompany him on the trip. He gives her a quick kiss, caresses her head, and, turning out the light, leaves.

IV

The streets are still somewhat dark when Guido's large Cadillac comes out of the garage. They are nearly deserted. The car stops at a lit-up gas station, and Guido has his tank filled. Then he goes to the telephone. Rapidly he dials the same number as before and waits nervously. Again the phone rings several times. Finally, however, someone answers. He hears the warm, drowsy voice of a woman.

"Anita? . . . Why didn't you answer? . . . I called an hour ago . . . . Where were you?"

Guido's tone is brisk, almost authoritarian. In spite of this, however, the voice on the other end remains calm and cordial. The voice has a note of surprise in it, but only a little bit, and warmth, despite the interrupted sleep.

"I was asleep. . . . When I'm sleeping, I don't hear any-thing. . . . What time is it? . . . Is it really you, Guido? How are you?"

"Get up and get dressed. . . . I'm coming over to pick you up in ten minutes. . . . We're going away. . . . Do you hear me? . . . Did you understand what I said?"

There is a pause at the other end. "Did you understand?" Guido repeats. "Get dressed. Put some things in a suitcase. . . . We'll be gone for a couple of days. . . . Five minutes and I'll be at your place." Then with his face shining and his voice a little hoarse, but joyful, Guido adds, "You mean very much to me."

Now the Cadillac crosses rapidly the still semideserted city. The light of the dawn increases. The street lights go off suddenly. The first trucks of the morning begin to roll. We see the majestic façades of the churches and the baroque palaces in the unreal, dawn light. Guido's car passes through a tree-lined section of the city, a section with large tenements like prisons, and a new section still under construction. Finally, Guido pulls up at the front door of a building that has just been unlocked for the day.

At a door on the seventh floor, Guido waits a long time, ringing several times, until someone opens the door for him.

Anita had gone back to sleep. Like a drowsy child, she is still lying on the bed now, half-asleep and half-awake. She is a young woman with a rich, full body. As Guido looks down at her in her sleepiness with its childlike and animal qualities, his state of anxiety melts away into delight. He laughs and shakes her. With his hands, he touches her shoulders and arms playfully. Anita lets him do what he wants, with a smiling and playful condescension on her part that is not passivity, but more nearly the loving patience of a mother toward the inopportune tricks of her little boy.

At last Anita gets up. Guido rummages in her bureau drawers to hurry the preparations. Only now that she is on her feet does Anita ask, without too much curiosity, "What do you have in mind? . . . I have to go to the office this morning."

"I'll arrange a medical excuse for you. . . . Two days only. . . . Come on, quick. . . . Hurry!"

Guido's overbearing exuberance leaves no opportunity, even for an instant, for Anita to say no. Once he has made a decision, all people and all things become for Guido instruments to be used at any cost and by any means. Only the genuine zest for life at the bottom of his colossal egotism justifies this aspect of his character and makes it bearable. His zest is contagious. It sparkles.

Anita is in the process of getting dressed now. Nothing ever knocks her off balance, not even the confusion of an unexpected awakening. Everything amuses her, especially if it is a surprise and involves a certain amount of chaos. Skip out on work, leave with Guido, a two-day trip. . . . Very well. . . . She does not even wonder where Guido wants her to go. . . . It is time to leave and she is still sleepy. . . . Nothing is ready. . . . She was planning to go to the movies that evening. . . . Very well, let's go, then. . . .

"It has been a long time since I've seen you," Anita observes without a trace of reproach in her voice. She jokingly gives Guido's arm a sharp pinch and looks at him with dancing eyes as a woman does when she likes a man and is disposed to do anything for him.

Guido drags Anita and her suitcase down the stairs. He settles her and her suitcase in the car with the same amount of care for each and drives off.

Anita allows herself to fall back on the cushions with a feeling of bliss as if she were in her own bed again. She closes her eyes and drifts back toward sleep. Almost immediately, however, Guido shakes her. "Get down. Put your head down," he says hurriedly. "My brother-in-law lives around the corner here."

Understanding the situation, Anita ducks down obediently and tries to get out of sight.

"Lower. Get down lower," Guido insists. Half-jokingly and half-seriously, he presses her head down, forcing her to double up.

Anita's large body creaks from the effort to hide. Yet when she reemerges in the seat later, she utters a sigh of satisfaction without any trace of resentment. Tilting her beautiful head back, Anita lets it slide onto Guido's shoulder, and she closes her eyes again.

The car leaves the city and speeds over an asphalt road among fields still veiled with mist. On the horizon the big, reddish ball of sun comes up.

V

At sixty miles per hour the Cadillac glides along the Cassia highway north of Rome. The highway is as smooth as a race track. Seated at the wheel, Guido sneaks continual glances at Anita who sleeps next to him. Her hair has become unfastened and covers half her face. In the abandonment of sleep, her large, soft body rocks with the movement of the car. Her blouse, which is stuck back against the leather seat, reveals in innocent shamelessness her throat, shoulders, and breasts.

All of a sudden, Guido brakes the car. It almost skids off the road.

Anita wakes up with a start, frightened. Guido pounces on her and kisses her on the neck and breasts. With patience and with a joyous look in her eyes still puffy from sleep, Anita permits him to continue. "What has come over you all of a sudden?" she asks in a tranquil tone.

Without answering, Guido goes on kissing her greedily. Anita looks around her at the rolling countryside and the distant hills. "Where are we?" she asks, still a little drowsy.

When the Cadillac starts off again, Anita picks up her pocketbook calmly, takes out her mirror, comb, and lipstick, and fixes herself up a bit. At the same time, she looks around, and, little by little as she wakes up more, she becomes aware of what is happening: the driving, the countryside, and the trip without an announced destination.

"Faster, faster," Anita cries joyfully to Guido.

As Anita's face lights up more and more with ingenuous pleasure over the trip, Guido's face grows darker. He knows that he should tell Anita the reason for the journey. The obligation to explain weighs heavily on him. It is a nuisance to him. More than that, the explanation would strike cords in him that he would rather leave untouched. But, finally, Guido decides that he must give the explanation, and so he begins to do it in a bored, hard-boiled, and roundabout way.

For Anita, however, the trip is nothing more than a vacation that has suddenly made her happy. With her joy comes a certain egotism. "I'm hungry," she announces, cutting off Guido's explanation. "I'm fainting with hunger. You didn't allow me any time to have breakfast this morning."

Guido gives up his attempt to speak seriously with Anita about his reason for the trip. Her joyfulness is infectious. And Guido realizes now that he, too, is hungry. At this hour, on a long trip, hunger is a delightful thing. He feels a tremendous, egotistical hunger like the ravenous desire for food that teenagers have.

Honking loudly and continously, Guido turns off the Cassia highway and drives at full speed into a narrow street of the small town of Sutri.

VI

A breakfast worthy of paradise is laid out: smoked ham, fried eggs, fava beans, pecorino and caciotta cheese, apples, strawberries, and Orvieto wine. Guido and Anita seem half-intoxicated. They are happy and insatiable. They are eating as if this were the first time in their lives they had ever eaten.

It has been many months, perhaps even years, since Anita has had such a nice vacation. This trip is all the more appealing to her because of its unexpectedness and its adventurous quality. She is inebriated with it. She speaks whatever comes into her head, and everything she says sounds cheerful, pretty, and amusing.

"What came over you this morning?" she asks Guido gaily. "It has been more than a month since I've seen you." Then Anita laughs and bites into a juicy peach.

"What about you?" answers Guido lightly. "I haven't asked you yet why you came with me?"

Anita falls silent. She seems a little confused, like a child caught in a mistake. She chews her peach for a moment, and then, looking Guido straight in the eye, she tells him with a sudden, laughing boldness, "Because I like you."

VII

Capranica, Viterbo, and Vetralla. The car moves toward the north. It has left the Cassia highway again and weaves through secondary roads getting farther and farther into the heart of the Apennine region. Now there comes into view in front of the car a long, narrow town clinging halfway up the side of a hill, overlooking a sheer ravine.

"Where are we?" asks Anita excitedly.

The car turns off onto the road that goes up into the center of the town and then onto the main street that traverses the length of the town. In the sunny noon hour the streets are almost empty. There are only a few old women in the streets and some schoolchildren loitering on their way home to play.

The Cadillac reaches the far end of the town. Suddenly the houses give way to a green clearing that offers a grand view of the surrounding hills and valleys.

Guido opens the car door excitedly, gets out, and runs across the clearing toward a path that goes along the side of the hill.

Amused and a little bit alarmed, Anita follows him, at a run, too. "Wait for me. . . . Guido, where are you going?" she cries after him gaily.

"Come on! Come on!" Guido shouts back from a distance.

The path winds along the sunny, green side of the hill, and after a small twist it leads up to a ledge over a short drop. Beyond, we can make out another hill rising up in the middle of a plain that stretches out for a great distance and vanishes finally into a sea of slopes and ridges. On the crest of the hill is a dark, hazy cluster of houses, which seems painted on a gauzelike material. . . .[3]

This town has been abandoned for more than three hundred years. A long, almost crumbling bridge leads into it. Guido runs

---

[3] I have inserted the ellipsis marks here to indicate the passage of time necessary for Guido and Anita to get from their vantage point to the bridge leading to the town on the far-off hill. It seems probable that Fellini would have achieved the transition through a dissolve in the film.

onto the bridge, and then after a few strides he stops. The bridge is almost without parapets, and it is full of holes. It is suspended above a chasm. Caught in an attack of vertigo, Guido is afraid to continue. But Anita, with the confidence and agility of a highwire artist, passes him and flies across the bridge.

Wiping away a cold sweat, Guido gropes along after her and reaches the other side. By now, however, Anita is scrambling up the steep, stony, little street that leads into the town. The girl is caught up in a kind of ferocious bliss that comes both from her love of adventure and discovery and from her delight in showing up Guido.

The town is completely empty. The narrow streets with uneven paving mount toward the sky. Long rows of houses heaped one on another are immersed in an absolute silence. Some of these houses are intact. Their doors and shutters are closed as if the inhabitants have left only temporarily. Other houses are almost in complete ruin with their doorways and windows staring out like empty eyeglasses.

Now we discover a little piazza with the church and a small villa of a noble family with only the external walls standing, and then we see the main street, which is like a crumbling and deserted alley, with the little town hall on it.

Anita runs shouting and laughing through the almost chilling, abandoned place. She is filled with the childish, sacrilegious desire to spread her joy and energy throughout the town. Guido follows her. As opposed to Anita, he feels subjugated by the spell of the funereal silence. Anita's flagrant gaiety offends him, and it frightens him a little. She runs on in front of him, having taken off her shoes in order to move better on the uneven paving. Anita doesn't want to let Guido catch up with her yet. She is looking for a place where it would be pleasant to stop and make love. Anita enters one of the houses, hesitates in the entry hall, runs to the upstairs rooms, appears at a window, and calls out. Leaving the house, she ventures into some animal sheds and into some little vegetable gardens overrun with weeds and dotted with skeletal trees. Finally, she reaches the far end of the town, which looks out on the immense plain below. Here some grass terraces, held up by small, primitive, circular walls, descend almost perpendicularly toward the plain. Anita scrambles down the terraces. Guido joins her at the bottom one, whose little wall perpendicular to the plain looks out on emptiness. The grass is thick and warm. Anita stretches out anxiously on it. . . .

VIII

Now it is almost evening. Lights shine from the farmhouses scattered through the hills. The Cadillac moves along with speed, and suddenly it comes to a crossroads. Which way to go? Anita would like to go right. Guido wants to go left. Anita takes a firm stand. They argue cheerfully and end by throwing fingers for odds or evens. Anita wins, and they go to the right, as chance has dictated.

Later, the car runs through an enchanted landscape. We see meadows sprinkled with lines of little trees and encircled by soft, serene hills. The evening sky is clear. And we can make out distant and mysterious rows of lights.

As they move deeper into this countryside, Guido seems to become bewitched. His sensual, passionate drive subsides. He appears lost in serious thought. Not caught in such a spell, Anita is even happier than before. Her innocent, animal vivacity contrasts with Guido's sober meditativeness.

Gradually, Guido begins to recognize places they pass. Here is that particular farmhouse, and there is that thicket. . . . The hills around them are those very gentle ones that stretch from Arezzo to Sansepolcro. Guido feels a mysterious happiness. He knows now where he is going and what he wants to show Anita, but he says nothing to her.

At a farmhouse Guido calls out for the female custodian for a church. She has a little boy clinging to her skirt. She is troubled that the evening has grown dark. Guido, however, is persistent.

Followed by the custodian and the little boy on foot, Guido drives the car farther on. Then he climbs out with Anita close behind him.

In a hollow of a hill near its top are a low, crumbling wall and a little gate. The group passes through the gate. In the last light of the evening, we can make out a small, charming, somewhat scraggly cemetery. Gaily Guido and Anita with the woman and the child behind them approach a chapel that is also crumbling.

The inside of the chapel is nearly pitch black. We can see just barely that the far wall has a fresco on it. Helped by the little boy, the woman bustles about, chattering brusquely and protectively in her clear Aretine dialect,[4] for the two outsiders have come to admire "her" masterpiece. Within an old, small altar covered with dust is a bunch of candles. One by one, the old woman lights them all. She sets two in the candelabra beneath the fresco and gives others to everyone to hold. The child stands on the altar and illuminates the top part of the fresco with his candle. In the weak, flickering light of the candles, a maternity scene by Piero della Francesca is revealed. The Madonna has a childlike quality. She is a young, inexperienced mother with her reddish hair drawn back, with her eyebrows depilated, and with a very soft, sad smile on her lips.

"Do you like it?" Guido asks Anita. He takes an excited, aesthetic delight in the fresco. Anita nods her head yes, but she doesn't understand his aesthetic response very well. She makes the sign of the cross, because for her the important thing is that she is in church.

IX

Once again Anita is hungry. She has the same ravenous hunger she had in the morning. Guido also finds himself longing

---

[4] The Aretine dialect is spoken around Arezzo in Tuscany and is considered one of the best of the Italian dialects. Perhaps more important, however, is the possibility that the dialect (as well as the landscape near Arezzo) would indicate to an Italian audience that Guido and Anita are now moving gradually east toward the Adriatic coast, where Fano is.

for a meal. The excitement of the adventure has seized them again. They crave something unusual . . . some small, but joyful delights. However, the time is rather late. Arezzo is far away, and their hunger is urgent, their whimsical desire high.

"May we eat with you?" Guido asks the custodian. "No matter what you have. No matter what the price."

Brusquely, but cordially and a little uncertainly, the woman offers the two travelers the hospitality of her poor home. The little boy exults over the novelty of the event. . . .

Salami, cheese, eggs, salad, peaches, apples, and wine from a cask. Guido and Anita eat voraciously with an appetite that seems to come from the heart. Around them are the daughters and nieces of the custodian, some eating with their plates on their knees, some sewing, and others just passing the time. They are girls from thirteen to twenty years of age. The only male in the house is the little boy. All the other males have gone out, the older ones to the tavern and the younger ones to the movies or to the feast in the nearby town.

It is the Night of San Giovanni.[5] The night is soft and deep. In the darkness outside the house, the countryside reverberates with distant voices and sighs and the yelps of dogs.

The girls of the farmhouse are mysteriously excited. It seems there is something they want to do, but they are embarrassed to do it with the two visitors present. At the same time, however, with the mother as their leader, they take advantage of the absence of men and surrender to a kind of mad joy. The woman draws more wine, and all the girls drink, laughing shyly and boldly, until they become a little tipsy. Then they make a decision. They take a jug that is full of water and pour in the white of an egg. One after another, the girls shake the jug.

On the Night of San Giovanni the girls are accustomed to perform these magic rites in order to see into the future. From the

---

[5]The feast of St. John the Baptist, patron saint of Florence, is on June 24. As observed in this rural Tuscan area, it seems to function mainly as a Midsummer's Night fertility celebration.

shape the egg white takes in the water, they can foretell if they will get married within the year and can see whom they will marry.

Intent mainly on their supper, Guido and Anita, nevertheless, follow these activities with some amusement and curiosity.

Suddenly the girls leave the room. A bit drunkenly, the mother hurls comic rebukes after the "crazy girls" and forces the little boy who wants to follow them to remain with her.

A period of profound silence ensues. The mother bustles about the kitchen in good humor, and the little boy plays.

A fierce longing for Anita comes over Guido again. Ignoring the presence of the woman and the child, he begins to compliment Anita and to tell her of his craving for her.

With a rosy glow from the trip, the fresh air, and the food, Anita looks marvelous. She listens to Guido contentedly. She is half-drunk from the light wine, and she laughs happily, strongly, and even a bit bawdily.

Now, in a mysterious manner, the girls make us aware of their presence again. First we hear voices, then smothered laughter, and then names being called: Inez! Maria! Finally the girls come down from the second floor of the farmhouse and go off toward a meadow behind the house.

"Mad, crazy girls," the mother mumbles to herself.

Guido and Anita are filled with irresistible curiosity. They want to see what is going to happen and rise to follow the girls. But the woman of the house, embarrassed, objects. The lady may go after the girls, she tells them, but not the man. Without waiting for Guido's reaction, Anita bursts out of the kitchen and runs toward the dark meadow.

Surprised and displeased, Guido remains behind and stares after Anita as she races off, trailing her slightly bawdy laughter behind her. She disappears beyond the first twisted apple and cherry trees of the farm in the moonlight. Again Guido starts to go toward the mysterious area of the farm, but the woman restrains him a second time. She is still a little embarrassed, and yet she also seems amused in the way a naughty child might be.

"On the Night of San Giovanni, the girls have to do these foolish things," she cackles to Guido. It is obvious that she wants to blurt out everything to Guido and have a good laugh over the girls' activities, but there is a little boy present and so she breaks off, putting her hand over her mouth to stifle her laughter.

Then she confides in a low voice, "They have gone to roll around naked in the dew on the grass of San Giovanni out in the meadow." Chuckling, the woman returns to the kitchen.

Guido and the little boy remain in the farmyard. They are two males excluded by the group of women. A kind of complicity springs up between them. Excited and embarrassed, they exchange confidences, trying to avoid the dangerous subject of the girls or else alluding to it in a joking way. All the while they can hear the voices of the girls shouting and laughing in the distance.

At the end of a row of interlaced fruit trees, a broad field of alfalfa opens out and vanishes from sight into the white light of the moon. A figure comes out from a tangle of two or three cherry trees and runs in the open over the thick mat of alfalfa. Another girl follows her, and then another. They chase each other playfully, plunge down onto the grass, and then disappear again behind the trees.

Now, a few at a time, the men of the house return. First come the older ones from the tavern, a little tipsy: the old grandfather, the father, and the uncle. These are hard, creased, sturdy men. Their faces are flushed from the wine and the smoke in the tavern. They stumble into Guido, standing in the yard in his slightly embarrassing situation. They greet him cautiously, and then behind his back they ask the mother why he is there. They don't understand her explanation fully, but they are willing to suspend judgment on the matter. In fact, the novelty of his presence seems to appeal to them.

Meanwhile, the young women continue frisking nude in the meadow. The men call to them in their hoarse voices, using colorful Tuscan words. The girls linger for a little while, answering the men from afar in shouts and bursts of laughter that can just barely be heard. At last the girls return. They have not put all their clothes back on yet, and they are still wet from the dew. The girls seem as proud and happy with their antics as they seem embarrassed and frightened by what they have done.

Triumphant in beauty among them is Anita. She is wet, and her hair is ruffled. Instead of decreasing her intoxication, the running in the meadow has increased it. She is caught up in an almost frantic gaiety. She feels at home among these people.

Her gaiety increases even more as the young men return excited from the dance or festival where they were. They are very young and boyish. They roar up on old, dilapidated motorbikes. One has an accordian strapped on his shoulders. A new round of introductions takes place quickly. Immediately the young men become part of the general gaiety. They have caught at once the feeling of celebration at the farm. The one with the accordian begins to play. The older people, including Guido, are now left somewhat out of the festivities. The younger people begin to dance, brothers with sisters and male cousins with female cousins. Several of the girls dance with each other. Overwhelmed with delight, Anita begins to dance energetically with a young man as if she had lost her mind.

The woman of the house passes around the fiasco of wine again, and everyone drinks. Anita grows still more excited. She has almost completely lost control of herself. Guido tries to restrain her, but her response is to seize his hands and force him to dance with her. Guido tries to pull back, but he isn't able to. Anita is very strong, and, impassioned by the wine, she holds onto Guido and makes him follow her moves. Then she loses patience with him when he stumbles and ends with a pratfall amid the whoops of laughter of the others. Anita's raucous laugh is the loudest of them all.

Without a partner now, Anita goes to the grandfather, who is still as strong as an oak and seems something of a sly old rascal. The young people are enormously amused, but with a light touch

of embarrassment. The older people, however, are not amused in
the least. Their faces darken as they watch the explosive movements of this wild animal, so marvelous and dangerous, who has
ended up in their home. Who knows what thoughts pass through
the hard heads of these older family members!

At the height of the celebrating, the grandfather and then the
mother begin to give orders for going to bed. The girls pretend not
to hear the orders for a while, but finally they give in. Still shouting
and laughing, they go off to their upstairs bedroom. The males are
allowed to be more autonomous, and they linger on for a while.

Too happy to recognize the little scandal she has caused,
Anita is surprised by this sudden defection. However, she does
not completely lose her joyful impetuousness. There is a touching
quality to it that comes from her unconcealed impudence and
from the emerging earthiness of an uneducated woman who may
be, after all, somewhat loose.

Suddenly, Anita runs off again toward the meadow. This
time there is no reason for Guido not to follow her. He has been
watching the excesses of his companion with more irony than
worry. Precisely because her actions have been so extravagant,
they have further stirred up his senses, which had already been
excited by his day of love with Anita, and so he races after her.

Laughingly, Anita disappears among the apple and cherry
trees with Guido behind her. Then she reaches a place where she
had probably been with the girls. Intoxicated then, she has had a
brief taste of their game. Still intoxicated now, she repeats the
game delightedly, childishly, and provocatively in front of
Guido. Anita strips off her clothes and begins to roll again, nude,
on the heavy dew of the grass of San Giovanni as if she were a colt
in a pasture or a dolphin in the sea.

X

Clearly there is something more to Anita than Guido knew
previously. From the first moments, their trip together, which he

had organized suddenly and brazenly, has been more cheerful, adventurous, and enchanting than he could have imagined in his wildest dreams. Now, however, things seem to Guido to have become more serious. He began to realize this during the evening in the farmhouse while he watched the antics of the tipsy Anita with a certain detachment. Something seemed to take Anita violently away from his reach. She appeared independent and mysterious. Her beauty, which increased in her delight over the vacation trip, seemed to explode into the outward form of her dance among the farmers and her nude romp on the grass. She was like an apparition. In addition, her inner simplicity as an uneducated, somewhat earthy woman appeared to burst out in a mixture of innocence and coarseness, of purity and immodesty, and of freshness and excess.

The car speeds along in the fresh sunshine of the morning. A very soft breeze blows in through the open windows. As the car advances, the landscape becomes higher and quieter. The solitude is almost Alpine. No longer do we see towns, houses, or human beings. We see only clouds and humps of mountains.

Guido and Anita feel deliciously alone in the world. They continue their trip in a northerly direction without an apparent destination. The tone of their trip changes a little bit now in the freshness and solitude of the morning. Lacking in guile as she is, Anita puts her cards on the table. She tells Guido that she had followed his activities from afar in the papers and on the radio during the month or so when he didn't call. Without being intimidated by his achievements, she is full of admiration for Guido's fame and success. He, on the other hand, seems embittered by his material and intellectual achievements, which give him no pleasure. He takes his material success for granted now, and his intellectual success seems to him to lack permanence and solidity in the torn, factious, skeptical world of today. But Guido is moved very much by Anita's candid interest, by her lack of sophistication, by the certitude she possesses, and by her self-consistency.

The car approaches the gorge of Furlo.[6] The mountains become higher. They appear dark against the clear morning sky. The weather is cool. There is not a house or a human being to be seen.

After a curve in the road on the chipped-into slope of a mountain, something new comes into view—some men and some parked trucks. The Cadillac comes up to this work site at full speed. A man waves a red flag, signaling the car to stop.

Leaning out of the window, Guido asks, "What's going on?"

"We're going to blast," answers a workman cheerfully.

The place is wrapped in a profound silence. The workers are spread out on the steep slope, some near a truck and others seated on blocks of limestone here and there. None of them wishes to disturb the silence. The tension of the waiting produces a mood that is almost magical.

Some of the workers are old men creased with wrinkles. Their skin has been burnt by the sun and chafed by the cold. Others are still young. Their boyish faces are creased by fatigue and late-night parties. These young workers, however, are full of the quiet forcefulness and the potential for violent action that humble people have. They have noticed the lady in the car and stare at her insistently. Perhaps it is only in Guido's imagination, but there seems to hover, barely perceptible in the air, the possibility of a challenging act—a leer, a whistle, or a whispered obscene remark. The boldest of the young workers begins to approach the car and look in with a certain brashness. Then they sit down on the edge of the road or else stretch out on the ground with an animal-like laziness such as cheerful hobos might have. In the insolence with which they look at Anita, there may be the very old and barely conscious acrimony of the poor against the rich, in this case, the possessor of a luxurious car.

---

[6] The gorge of Furlo is near the Adriatic coast and Fano. It would now be obvious to an Italian audience that Guido and Anita are making their way toward Fano, despite the apparently random course of their journey to this point.

Guido is very uneasy. Anita, on the other hand, is not aware of any tension and is perfectly at ease, as if everything were normal. She takes advantage of the halt to get out of the car and stretch her legs. It isn't that she wishes consciously to arouse further the already excited workers, but perhaps she acts from the instinctive coquetry of a sexually healthy and extremely sensual woman.

Certainly she doesn't know it, but she acts with the same natural disregard of her beauty that she acted with the night before. At the most, she has only a secret, feminine awareness of the impact she makes. Again she seems to Guido to have an exciting, submerged earthiness in her.

Anita allows the young workers to strike up conversation with her. They are respectful and friendly, although inwardly they retain some violent, menacing wishes. Standing in the midst of these workers, Anita is outlined against the mountain and the sky in all her animal beauty.

Guido gets out of the car also and tries to hide his uneasiness behind a mask of cordiality. He offers the men cigarettes and chats with them.

Anita is thirsty. A young worker passes her a fiasco filled with water. In the midst of the camaraderie, she holds the bottle high and pours the contents into her mouth. The water comes out of the neck of the bottle and runs down her throat, between her breasts and beneath her dress.

The waiting for the explosion continues. The silence in the valleys and the gorges seems to increase during the waiting. Then we hear voices. The foremen are issuing orders. The workers no longer joke. They line up on the slope of the mountain to watch. Almost fearfully, Guido and Anita sense that the blast is imminent.

In the deep, clear quiet of the sky, we see the serene mountains with their peaks, furrows, and fissures like enormous gray and brown wrinkles. Then the explosion comes with brutal suddenness. There is something sinister or unexpectedly excessive about the blast. A series of echoes follows the explosion. They wind among the mountains with an interminable rumble. It seems as if an entire mountain has come down in a landslide. A large, heavy cloud of dust rises now and spreads slowly throughout the valley.

Guido is seized with an urgent feeling of haste. He doesn't want to stay here among the workers for another moment. Having watched the spectacle of the explosion, the workers are coming back toward Anita with their silent, threatening lust. Guido pays no attention to the foreman who tells him that it might be dangerous to resume driving right away. Guido makes Anita get back in the car, and he drives off furiously.

                                    XI

Guido is overcome with a mysterious, inner rage. With inexplicable spitefulness, he begins to attack Anita, almost enjoying the taste of his harsh words. Without a logical motive or apparent justification, he condemns her behavior with the workers. He reproaches her and her kind of person with a burning rancor. On the one hand, his words, stemming from his irrational need to vent his feelings, are senseless, and, on the other hand, they are lucid and penetrating. He calls her a whore. In reality he is shaken by a terrible jealousy that is as violent as it is sudden. It explodes like the dynamite charge.

Anita listens to him without daring to breathe, but also without losing her composure. Perhaps with her instinct, she senses what is beneath this explosion of jealousy and irritation.

What explodes in Guido is, at bottom, love, the pain and complexity love implies, and the sense of crisis love brings to real life and dreams. The innocent cause of this suffering is Anita with her devotion, magnificence, strength, and resignation.

The enormous cloud of dust continues to spread. It covers the entire area of the mountain ahead through which the road curves gently. As the car enters this dust, which is like a thick fog,

Guido has to slow down to the speed of someone on foot. In this kind of darkness, Guido's rage reaches full force.

When the cloud of dust thins out a little, the infuriated and exasperated Guido orders Anita to leave the car. Without speaking, she climbs out as if she were obeying the whim of a child. She is calm and even dignified. She waves good-by to him.

The desperate Guido drives off without understanding fully what he has done. Because of the cloud of dust that continues to swirl around the car, he must proceed slowly. After less than a mile, however, Guido brakes the car violently and turns it around.

By now, the air has cleared. The sun is shining very brightly. From distant, invisible towns, we hear the noon bells ringing. Guido retraces his route quickly. He discovers Anita seated on a low wall with her pocketbook at her feet. She is calmly filing her nails. Intent on her work, she doesn't raise her head. When she decides finally to look at Guido behind the wheel of the stopped car, she smiles.

XII

Guido and Anita are getting near the sea and Fano. Memories of the buried past rush back to Guido, and thoughts of his father surge painfully and vividly into his mind.

He stops the car sharply in front of a small bar in a little town with the excuse of getting them something to drink. However, he goes directly to the telephone.

It takes a long time to place a call to his father's town. Anita cannot help realizing that something is going on that is profoundly important to Guido. But Guido avoids giving her an explanation. He no longer has the courage. And she doesn't press him.

Finally, Guido's call goes through. He learns from his family that his father is much better and seems out of danger.

Relieved, he tells Anita now the reason for the trip. He speaks with optimism and good humor in light of the recent good news. Now, however, he is uncertain whether or not to go to his home.

Guido is pushed into paying the visit by Anita. She can't conceive of anyone doing otherwise. Anita has suddenly become a different, more serious person. She is full of a dignity Guido didn't know she had. Anita asks Guido why he hid the truth until now. In her voice, there is a tone of surprised and sad reproach that strikes Guido forcefully and perplexes him.

Slowly they drive on side by side, serious and withdrawn from each other. All at once, they find themselves in front of the sea. The place is strange. It is one of those places where children play, with the land dried out from the saltiness, but thick with undergrowth and dotted with small vegetable gardens. The grass stretches down almost to the edge of the sea. Close by the little grassy beach runs a railroad track without much of an embankment. The place is deserted except for some run-down shacks. Far off, we can see the large buildings on the outskirts of Fano. Some children are playing on the grass, but they are so distant they seem to be in another life.

Guido and Anita leave the car and make their way from clearing to clearing among the brambles, the prickly bushes, and clumps of nettles until they reach the grassy beach. In the shelter of the stunted vegetation, they lie down, half on the grass and half on the sand. And in this bewitched spot outside of time and the seasons, they hold each other tightly, lost in a passion that shuts out the rest of the world.

XIII

It is only a mile or so to Fano. The road runs along the seacoast. Inside the car Guido and Anita are silent. Guido has lost his customary liveliness as a conversationalist who can be both eager and a little harsh, both subtle and childish. Now he is quiet as if constrained by deep emotions that he didn't anticipate. Anita respects her companion's silence. Discreetly, however, she tries to break into the silence from time to time and asks Guido a few questions. Detached and distracted as he is, he answers her briefly or not at all.

Meanwhile they are entering the outskirts of Fano. The features of Guido's face and his gestures reveal now an emotion in him that approaches anguish. He recognizes some landmarks he had forgotten and some views of the landscape he had not seen for many years.

Now we see the beach, the beachfront promenade of the outskirts, rows of cottages, small hotels, and children's seaside summer camps.[7]

Guido is hardly aware of Anita's presence now. Sometimes, when an emotion is so strong that he can't hold it in or when a memory has to be expressed, Guido speaks out loud, but he does not address his words to Anita, who listens to him in silence.

Seeing a small hotel facing the sea, Guido brings the car to an abrupt halt. He gets out of the car and drags Anita out with him. He removes her suitcase from the car's trunk. They enter the hotel, and Guido signs Anita into a room. Then he leaves the hotel, slides back into the Cadillac, and drives off, almost without waving good-by.

XIV

Guido's old house stands on one of those interior streets of seaside towns, which, even though they are old streets, have something fresh, new, lively, and also profoundly melancholic about them. Actually, the house sits right on the corner of the main street that runs toward the station and the sea.

It is a two-story house like the others on the street. In front it has a small garden, which is somewhat stunted by the saltiness of the soil. A gravel path runs through the garden to the house. Guido stops his car in front of the house. The car is covered with dust from the long trip. Guido climbs out of it.

The gate to the garden is open. The house itself looks empty.

---

[7] These camp buildings are for children from the interior who would not have the opportunity to come to the beach in the summer if it were not for the camps. Usually these camps are sponsored by the church or the government.

The windows are open also, and the front door is ajar. Guido goes up the old stairs almost at a run.

On the landing, as if by chance, Guido meets his sister Gina. Hurriedly and in silence, they embrace. Their greeting is not important at the moment. Although it has been many years since they have seen each other, they reestablish their former rapport at once.

Gina leads Guido to his father's room. There he finds his mother, who also embraces him hurriedly and in silence, and the maid. Guido's father is stretched out on a small bed. He seems lost to the world in a deep sleep. Watching him, along with the family, are two young doctors and the chief of staff from the hospital, a man extremely dignified and authoritative in appearance.

In the anxious, respectful silence of everyone, Guido steps forward to the bedside and leans over his father. Guido looks at him for a long time with a compassionate curiosity as if he were seeing him for the first time. The illness and the extreme weakness of the father, in effect, render the man disarmed. His face is white and bony. The father stirs, begins to pull out of his sleep, and opens his eyes. He stares blankly at Guido for a moment and then recognizes him. The father reacts with emotion somewhere between joy and distress. He fidgets on the bed, and then with a painful effort he rises up toward his son. "Guido," he murmurs, "now why did you go to all the trouble of coming?"

Upset by these words, Guido puts his hand on his father's shoulder, forcing him gently to lie back down. Guido is at a loss for words.

The chief of staff intervenes with a professional kind of good humor in an attempt to cheer the patient. As he speaks, the others in the room accord him the utmost respect. The emaciated mother looks at him with her large, grief-stricken eyes as if he were an oracle.

The mother can't hide an absurd hope in her eyes, nor can she hide the love and joy she feels at her son's homecoming. She takes Guido by the arm and leads him into the little kitchen. She is overcome with an unrealistic optimism. "I prayed so much," she tells her son. "I have prayed so much. . . ."

The mother speaks as if her words will gain validity once she says them to Guido and invokes him as a witness to them. She declares with a desperate certitude, "You will see that he will get well now that you are here."

One of the two young doctors comes into the kitchen. Hesitantly, with a faint, shy smile, he looks at Guido. The young doctor was a friend in elementary school days, and he reminds Guido about those days—the teacher, the desks, and the girls in the class. As the doctor talks on affectionately about the past, he reveals in his voice a certain timid admiration for a friend who has become a celebrity.

A shuffling of footsteps and a murmur of voices are heard now in the hall. The chief of staff is about to take his leave. Immediately everyone leaves the kitchen to see him out of the house. Full of the naïve veneration that the average person has for a doctor, Guido's mother hangs on the doctor's every word as if these words would save her from drowning, at least for a little while.

With a paternal air, the chief of staff does, in fact, give some words of encouragement to the women of the house. Then he takes Guido by the arm and descends with him into the garden in front of the house. The two men walk back and forth on the little path. Gravely the doctor speaks to Guido man to man. It is all too clear that the doctor is flattered and excited to be talking with a famous writer, and he tries to show off.

Meanwhile, the mother peeks surreptitiously out of a half-opened window. Only Guido is aware of her. From her vantage point, the mother watches all the movements of the men and attempts to overhear their words.

Although respected by the whole town, the chief of staff is a vain, silly old man. Talking with Guido, he adopts an inspired, divulgent tone. "You know," he instructs, "the heart is a mysterious muscle . . . a capricious one. . . . Indeed, it functions in the gray area where science borders on philosophy and medicine borders on art. . . ." Then in the intellectual language filled with obscure allusions that all the "great ones" use, the doctor passes to another subject.

Suddenly the doctor breaks off and looks into the eyes of his interlocutor with a certain fierceness. "What are they talking about in Rome?" he asks unexpectedly in his grave voice. "What is that Saragat doing?"[8] Then after commenting ominously about the politics of the Social Democratic party, the doctor takes his leave at last.

He walks out the gate and goes to his car. Before getting in, however, the doctor turns one last time and says paternally to Guido, "Keep your mother calm."

XV

Now a new hope has been kindled in Guido's mother and sister, and as a result of this Guido also feels optimistic. He has led his mother to believe that he departed only on the previous evening, because he had had things to do in Rome and that he drove through the night to reach Fano. His mother is worried that Guido has overexerted himself. She insists that he go rest for a while at the hotel where he has told her he took a room. "Papa seems so much better," she tells him. Allowing himself to be persuaded by his mother's affectionate insistence, Guido leaves.

Guido sets out on foot for the main street that goes to the station and the sea. His ostensible goal is the small hotel on the beach, but in reality he has no wish to go there. He no longer knows what he does want to do. At the same time he is getting caught up again in the everyday life of the town around him. He

---

[8] Giuseppe Saragat (born 1898) is a politician. He founded the Social Democratic party (PSDI) in 1949 and was president of the Republic of Italy from 1964 to 1971. At the time of this screenplay—1957—he was concerned with mending breaches among the various Socialist factions.

had forgotten what that life was like. Now, however, as memories flood back, the life of the town seems to Guido identical to the way it was before.

The day is one of those in which the light is so strong that it gives everything an insubstantial appearance. It seems to wash out the contours of everything. Guido hears cries and voices in the old dialect around him.

On the main street the traffic and the movement of people are intense, blurred, and lively. The shops for beach articles blaze with their bright colors in the violent light. Boys in shorts and sandals and perspiring women with shopping bags parade along the street.

Dazed by this rediscovered life, Guido enters a bar and orders a cappuccino. While he waits, Guido leans exhausted against the bar. His eyes, however, take in avidly all the gestures and all the details of the people and the scene around him.

All of a sudden Guido hears high-pitched, excited voices in the street outside. He goes to the door. A little way off is a taxi. The agitated driver is asking for information, but no one can help him. Then he drives forward and stops in front of the bar. "Is Guido in there?" he shouts into the bar.

Guido steps forward.

"Get back to your home as fast as you can," the driver tells him, and, putting the taxi in gear, he drives off without waiting for Guido's response. The taxi is soon lost from sight in the traffic and sunlight.

Guido sets off at a run toward his house. The one hundred yards that separate him from the gate of the garden he left such a short time ago seem to him now an immense distance.

And then he sees his sister in the window of the house waiting for him and gesturing to him. When he gets beneath the window at last, the frightened Gina calls out to him, "Hurry, Guido. . . . Papa is dead!" and then immediately she disappears from the window sill.

Guido runs up the stairs and enters the house.

This is one of those moments when reality seems to flicker. Suddenly every gesture, every movement, and every voice seem to be recast in an unknown form that the senses can absorb only in fragments. Extremely simple gestures acquire immense meaning, and very important things shrink and vanish from perception.

The maid passes in front of Guido. She cries more from fright than grief. The mother speaks from the kitchen in a voice that seems not to be hers. The anxiety in her voice is absurdly below what one would expect for the gravity of the moment and above what one would normally apply to the small detail she seizes on desperately. "Put the blue tie on him," she says, "the one he liked so much."

Torn by the words of his mother, Guido clamps his hands to his face so hard that he almost hurts himself. He goes into the small bedroom where his father died and finds women in the process of dressing him.

At this point, the telephone rings unexpectedly, absurdly, and hauntingly. Since no one else answers it, Guido forces himself to do it tremblingly.

The caller asks to speak with Guido's father. He says that he represents some manufacturers or dealers with business connections with the father. Guido doesn't understand exactly. He tells the caller that his father is not there. The caller, however, insists and says something about a lumber deal. Guido is forced to speak the words, "My father has died."

Meanwhile, relatives and good friends begin to arrive with mysterious promptness. An old friend of the father enters the house and goes directly to kneel by the bed without having the strength to say a word. Then arrive an uncle and a cousin whom Guido barely remembers. After them come an aunt and a young nephew whom Guido has never seen. Guido, however, recognizes with much emotion the family traits in the boy. He has the face and the eyes of the family. Next enters a relative whom Guido has not seen for so many years that he no longer recognizes him. Suddenly the face of Titta looms in front of him. Titta was Guido's best friend in childhood, the one to whom Guido was most closely tied. Now Titta has become beefy, red-faced, and somewhat gruff. The two friends embrace in silence. They suppress the words of cheerful surprise that they would have uttered in other circumstances.

Well informed on the etiquette of the occasion, the maid bustles up to Guido. She has the comical wisdom of a young girl who is destined to be a spinster. She tells Guido that he should notify the nuns about the evening vigil.

XVI

Guido is relieved to have an excuse to depart from the house and to have something to do. Beyond the gate of the garden, he sees his parked Cadillac, still covered with dust from the long journey with Anita. The trip seems to him now a very distant event that happened in another world. This is so much the case that he is astonished by the tangible evidence of the dust that blankets the car.

From a boy, Guido learns the nuns he seeks are not in their convent, but are in church.

The little church is modernistic in a pseudobaroque manner. It is illuminated brightly by lights and candles, in contrast to the fading light outside now. Except for a few old women in the back pews, the only ones in the church are the nuns. There are at least two dozen in the pews under the high pulpit.

In this pulpit we can see a friar from the waist up. He has a thick beard and bushy hair. He preaches by shouting and seething at those beneath him. The nuns listen to him intently and tremble like a flock of pigeons.

Guido approaches the nuns and tries to speak with various ones, but he is unable to succeed in diverting their attention from the edifying sermon. Finally, one nun tells him to speak to the mother superior and points her out.

The mother superior is a small nun who seems younger than the others. In fact, she is as minute and pretty as a little angel, although faded and somewhat haggard from a life without much joy in it. Guido goes near her and stares at her curiously. Perhaps he is being indiscreet, but perhaps he also enjoys embarrassing her a little bit. She is probably much embarrassed by his stare, but she hides her feelings in her silence. Guido speaks to her with extreme politeness and with the imperious self-assurance of a conqueror. He requests the nuns' presence at the evening vigil. The mother superior becomes more friendly, and in her faint smile we can detect perhaps a trace of innocent, childlike coquetry.

XVII

Guido feels as if he were living in a dimension of life that is removed from reality and logic. He doesn't know how to understand what is going on. Not only does he feel estranged now, but also he realizes that he has felt this way for many years. It is not just the emotional intensity of the moment that has made him feel disengaged from events around him.

Night falls gently, and the first lights of the town come on. The nuns arrive at the home of Guido's family. In their serene, unworldly manner, they begin to sing prayers. Their voices are very sweet, graceful, and angelic, although the nuns don't seem to intend to do more than perform their duty with utter simplicity.

Guido's mother sits silently by the bed in a heart-breaking, natural solemnity. She is lost in a mysterious calm. Like the nuns, she knows what she must do and how she must act.

As the evening progresses, other relatives who live outside the town arrive. With more calmness and composure, they reconstitute the scene of earlier in the day. There come uncles and cousins who have been forgotten by Guido or else are completely unknown to him. There are children who have been born and have grown in the years since Guido left home. In the expressions, the gestures, and the words of these relatives, we can make out beneath the grief of their mourning and the anguish over the death a certain profane curiosity about the famous relative, the prodigal son who has returned after so many years.

The maid, that poor soul who has no life of her own, informs Guido that they should provide a supper and that there is nothing in the house.

Again Guido is quite relieved to withdraw from the atmosphere of the house. He goes outside and gets into his dust-covered car.

A little later, he returns and piles up the things he has brought in the kitchen. He has gotten everything in the world: wine, chickens, and even a lobster.

When they are invited, the relatives come quietly to get something to eat. Impressed, they stand motionless before the table with the food spread on it. Most obviously awed are the children, who have not yet learned how to disguise their feelings. For them, the evening vigil is a kind of party, although a reserved and quiet one. With the hunger of innocent children and the discretion of those raised in the country, these sturdy, humble boys and girls eat heartily. It is a pleasure to watch them. They are full of gratitude for their rich and generous uncle.

Then the quietness and the anguish return. In the whole house the only sound is that of the nuns who murmur and sing their prayers.

A sudden tiredness comes over Guido. Up to now, he has been too keyed up to be aware of any weariness. Now the tiredness seems to make him go mad. He can no longer bear that quietness, those voices, and that atmosphere. Abruptly he decides to break away. He can hardly hold back his tears in saying good night to his mother.

Guido descends into the garden. In front of him, in a patch of light from a street lamp, is the car, white with dust. Wearily, he begins to climb into the car when a voice cries his name. It is his mother calling from the only low window opening onto the garden. She looks at him uncertainly. Wanting to express the enormity of her misery, which is, in fact, beyond human expression, she can only ask pathetically, "Guido, have you found out that papa died?" Choking on her tears, the mother cannot continue speaking. She nods good night and pulls back inside the house.

XVIII

We see the half-covered body of the sleeping Anita. Moonlight enters through the wide open window of her hotel room. The sea rumbles lightly. Anita's body in that light with that sound seems a marvelous apparition.

Guido stands on the threshold of the room for a long time looking at her. After awhile, however, he decides to awaken her. As soon as she opens her eyes and comes to her senses, Guido tells her that his father has died.

Anita says nothing. An expression of sorrow and compassion spreads over her face. Still without speaking, she rises, washes her face, puts on a slip over her almost nude body, and throws something over her shoulders. She advances toward Guido, and timidly, but with a sense of certainty about what she says and with a sincerity that astonishes Guido, she tries now to comfort him and bolster him. And she murmurs, in particular, about the grief Guido's mother must be feeling.

Guido, however, is not moved by Anita's efforts . He still has the feeling that everything is happening in another dimension.

"How old was he, your father?" Anita asks.

Guido can't answer the question, for he doesn't know his father's age.

"What, you don't know?" exclaims Anita, full of hurt astonishment.

"No, I don't know," Guido confirms.

Anita looks at him with an indescribable expression. Perhaps pity is the nearest approximation.

The night is warm. Guido and Anita go out on the balcony, which looks onto the sea in the moonlight. Very distinctly, they can hear the breathing of the sea.

Leaning on the wrought-iron railing, Guido relates the events of the day to Anita. He describes his impressions, his observations, and the details of all the events in such a way that they seem to be projected onto a screen. However, he becomes muddled and overwhelmed when he tries to analyze or explain the happenings.

To Anita, Guido appears inhuman. "You tell those things as if they were part of a story," she says, with an expression that now mingles grief with pity.

As Guido continues to talk of the events of the day, she interrupts him every now and then with the murmur, "Poor Guido."

Struck by her tone and her words, he asks, "Why poor Guido?"

Astonished, Anita stares at him. The meaning of her words and of her tone seems perfectly clear to her. She has no wish to explain her words and her tone, or maybe she does not know how to. In any case, she withdraws into the room instead of answering and finishes getting dressed.

Dawn is beginning. A streak of light appears on the calm horizon. The dawn, however, seems overcast and sad. The sea stands out clearly as an enormous, inert, gray sheet of water. Then the beach becomes clearly visible, and finally the road that comes down from the hills and follows the coastline can be seen.

A group of women on bicycles appears on the road, and then another group. The women carry vegetables, flowers, and huge bunches of camomile on their handlebars. Two or three of them sing some old, slightly bawdy folk songs, and the women call back and forth to each other.

The sun climbs higher. Its brightness, almost burning now, strikes everything beneath it. Dazed and worn out, Guido stretches out on the bed in the hotel room. In the strong morning light, he drops off into a blind slumber.

XIX

When Guido returns to his house, he finds a disturbing quality of serene normality about it now. The nuns left early in the morning. The front rooms are quiet and empty. In the kitchen the mother moves about calmly, making coffee in her usual way.

Guido has entered the house without making any noise. No one is aware of his presence. He goes softly into the small room where his father reposes. It seems to Guido that his father lies in the bed like a man sleeping late. This is the first time, now in the silence and solitude, that Guido has come face to face with his dead father.

At first, held back by an obscure fear, Guido contemplates his father from a distance. Then he moves forward, drawn by the calm, mysterious smile fixed on his father's face as if a mask had fallen away and the man were revealing defenselessly now an intimate secret he had concealed all his life. All at once Guido has the strange sensation that he sees himself in the body of his father. The feeling of complete detachment or estrangement from his father that he always felt in the past vanishes. Every part of that immobile body seems rooted in Guido. The hands are different, and the lines of the face, the ears and the forehead, all different. Yet the differences seem only variations of a certain theme or model.

For a long time Guido looks at his father. Then it seems to him that the inexorable immobility of the father has something of the eternal about it that cannot be born too long. Hurriedly Guido leaves the room and searches for his mother and sister.

They are awaiting him as women wait traditionally for the man of the house. Now he is the one with the indisputable right and duty to handle matters concerning the family. There is a great deal to be done: papers from city hall, funeral arrangements, and the selection of a tomb. Sitting in a corner of the kitchen between the table and the stove, Guido discusses these matters with the two women in a soft voice as if this kind of intimate, family discussion were normal. The result is that the painfulness of the subject matter is softened, which, in turn, renders the discussion almost surreal.

Then Guido departs from the house. He feels like a stranger in his hometown, and he needs advice. His mother wants him to obtain rights to a pleasant location in the cemetery for his father, and the procedures necessary for this are complicated.

All at once he remembers his old friend Titta who has become a lawyer and who is important in the town government. Guido decides to seek out his friend.

The waiting room is filled with farmers. The room reeks with barnyard smells. The farmers have placed straw baskets on the floor between their heavy shoes. Their faces have been baked by the sun and are full of suspicion and held-in aggressiveness.

Exuberantly and sonorously, Titta is arguing with a farmer as if the two of them were bargaining in the marketplace. Titta slaps the farmer on the back, shouts the same phrase at him three or four times, and pushes him brusquely toward the door. Titta makes a show of walking away from the farmer, but then turns back and asks one more time whether the farmer has taken him for an imbecile in asking for a year's work from him in exchange for two turkeys and a few eggs. Stubbornly the sly farmer continues to hold out toward Titta his basket of eggs and his two turkeys, pretending to believe that the lawyer refuses them only out of politeness.

Suddenly Titta becomes aware of Guido's presence and lets out a shout. Leaving the farmer standing there with his eggs and turkeys, Titta runs to Guido and embraces his friend. Immediately Titta becomes solicitous with genuine concern for Guido. The words he says to Guido about his father's death sound sincere, despite their colorful, provincial effusiveness.

When Titta learns that Guido needs his help, he dismisses his waiting clients rudely: "Get out of here. I'm busy this morning. . . . Out! . . . Out!. . ." Then he leads Guido into a little garden that encircles his house.

Holding Guido tightly by the arm, Titta speaks of childhood memories and of Guido's father. Through the reminiscences of this friend not seen for many years, Guido rediscovers with surprising vividness many events of the past that he had forgotten completely. Some events don't come back to him at all, despite Titta's attempts to invoke them, but Titta reminisces about these events with such liveliness and good humor that Guido ends up laughing heartily over them, nevertheless.

"Do you remember," asks Titta, "the whacks with the umbrella we got that afternoon? . . . Do you remember? When your father took his siesta, we used to take some change from his vest pocket for the movies. . . . And then that afternoon he pretended to be asleep . . . and when we were going through his pockets, he whacked us twice with the umbrella and called us thieves...."

In the back part of the garden, somewhat hidden behind a plant is an old man, Titta's father. "Papa," Titta calls. "It's Guido. Giovanni's son." But the old man slips farther into concealment as if he had not heard.

"He is still very upset," explains Titta. "Your father's death frightened him. They were the same age. They were friends. . . . Last night at the table, he wouldn't touch a thing. He just sat there all evening looking at the tablecloth and swearing every now and then."

Then Guido and Titta go together to the town hall. The old palace in the center of the sleepy, sun-drenched town is semideserted. Long, dusty, empty corridors, doors to the right and left, some building attendants, an office, a service window, a table, and a counter. As if he were in a gallery of old portraits, Guido sees faces of friends from his youth now changed by the years. Some of the friends have become gray and tired. Others are still lively and retain at least the pretense of youth. Loudly and happily, Titta informs them all that Guido has returned. At the moment of recognition, each one of the friends reacts with surprise and sincere delight, but these emotions are tempered for most of them by various kinds of instinctive timidity before a former companion who has become famous in Rome, and these emotions are dimmed appreciably for a few of them by unconscious pangs of envy.

Guido who notices all this immediately experiences a strange sense of uneasiness in meeting these companions who have stayed behind and grown old in offices of the provincial town. They are tied now and forever to an out-dated world that Guido has gone beyond and almost forgotten.

At the same time, from the conversations, there emerge again shared memories, and from the shared memories, in turn, emerges a certain, genuine feeling of togetherness. Since the memories concern juvenile adventures that have been built up over the years to the status of major historical events in the lives of these provincials, some of the group break out in laughter.

From a service window a man attracted by the voices sticks out his head. "Guido," he cries joyfully. It is the group comedian, the witty one who never failed to get a laugh from them with his antics. He had a restless, whimsical temperament. He was capable of any madcap adventure. And here he is now, penned up in the town hall like the others. Yet he is still as lively as ever, full of funny quips and outbursts of bawdy anecdotes. As soon as he sees Guido, he takes off in a rapid-fire string of jokes and causes the others to laugh uproariously, until Titta interrupts in his booming voice: "Hey, cut it out! . . . Guido's father has died."

Mortified, the group comedian breaks off immediately and becomes serious. "Jesus Christ, Guido," he murmurs, "my condolences."

Concerning the matters that Guido must settle, everyone offers opinions and advice: apply to such and such an office; file such and such a form. Several of the group set about at once to expedite things. Some write letters on his behalf.

Guido learns that he must obtain a design for the tomb and receive aesthetic approval for the monument. Titta advises him on whom to see: "Eugenio. . . . Do you remember him? He studied architecture, got his degree, and now is very highly regarded in town."

Eugenio is found in the Central Cafe. He has a pointed beard in the manner of a turn-of-the-century artist. His hair is grizzled. As he listens to Titta, Eugenio's eyes light up with joy. A commission for the cemetery monument for the family of the famous fellow-citizen who made good in Rome! Eugenio feels that his day has come at last. He nods vigorously and speaks loudly, addressing his remarks more to the cafe regulars at the surrounding tables than to Guido. Then Eugenio takes Guido by the arm and walks with him back and forth in the piazza as if Guido were a trophy to be displayed. Continuously Eugenio exclaims and gesticulates.

"It should be more like a home than a tomb," he says. "Leave it to me. . . . Your mother will be there all the time. I know her. I can see it now. . . . We'll need to have a bench. . . . And I would also have a little altar . . . with a chapel area around it, because your mother will want to have many masses celebrated there."

Around Guido and Eugenio, the group of people in the piazza begins to thin out. It is time for them to return home for the noon meal. With a kind of dreamy bewilderment, Guido watches the home-going ritual of the townspeople while he listens to Eugenio. The pattern of the town's daily life has become strange to him. He is a detached observer of it, but to some extent he also feels drawn back into it as a participant. He sees how the hours pass here and how the entire day slips by.[9]

XX

Toward evening Guido feels exhausted. Once again he realizes that he has forgotten completely about Anita. The thought of her flashes through his mind for a moment, and he feels a pang of tenderness mixed with annoyance. Then the thought of her vanishes again, cancelled out by the pressing urgency of things he must do.

Guido goes to get the nuns for the vigil of this second night and returns to his home with them.

Friends and relatives are taking their leave. The house empties slowly in a rustle of footsteps and a soft murmur of voices broken at intervals by the sobbing of a woman.

---

[9] There is no break in the typescript at this point, but I have chosen to show a division in order to make clear a passage of time between the noon ritual of the return home of the townspeople at the end of Section XIX and the beginning of evening at the outset of Section XX. Presumably Guido spends this afternoon making more funeral arrangements.

A large friar introduces himself to Guido and embraces him with a fatherly, sympathetic effusion that is a little too practiced. "I am Brother Elijah," he announces, trying to hold his booming voice down to a soft tone.

Guido doesn't know who Brother Elijah is and responds with a vague smile and an indefinite nod.

Holding Guido's arm in a viselike grip, the friar steers him toward the window and continues speaking as if he assumes that Guido knows all about him. While he talks, he looks around triumphantly, reminding Guido of the sculptor of the morning. But the friar, like the others of the town, seems also to have a sincere emotion beneath it all.

Gradually Guido begins to figure out that Brother Elijah was a close friend of his father. The friar represents a side of his father's life that Guido did not suspect. Guido had always thought his father had no religious concern. The father used to speak of priests and practicing Catholics with the joking derision of provincial free thinkers. And yet he chose a friend from among the ranks of the religious. This somewhat pompous friar had been his father's confidant!

From the room where the father lies come the voices of the nuns who have begun their soft singsong again.

At the doorway prior to leaving, the friar blesses his dead friend and murmurs to Guido, "Go to your mother. . . . Keep her company. . . . It has been a terrible day for her, today."

Now the house is quieter. Some of the people besides the friar have departed. Still present, however, are the nuns. The mother superior who had shone a bit with innocent flirtatiousness the day before in response to Guido's attentions has withdrawn to a state of resigned abstraction now that Guido has forgotten about her. The childlike voices of the nuns alternate in two parts, responding to each other in a soft monotone. The softness of their singing seems involuntary.

All those still in the house experience a sense of infinitude in their souls. Stillness and drowsiness pervade the house. The women move slowly through the rooms. Their steps hardly make noise. Their voices are soft and calm. Night advances with the ancient silence of the dark, heavy countryside around the provincial town. The ethereal chanting of the nuns and the flickering light of the candles beyond the door of the father's room hint of a mysterious and solemn presence.

Tonight Guido will sleep beside his mother. Not for an instant does he consider leaving her and returning to Anita. The large double bed is the only one available, and so for this night the mother and son will share it. The mother undresses behind the armoire and puts on a large, white cotton nightshirt of the kind popular thirty years earlier. She climbs into bed immediately. A slight embarrassment weighs on both of them. In silence Guido also undresses and then lies down in the place that was his father's.

Both the mother and the son are tired, but sleep does not come at once. They speak slowly and softly. Then they turn out the light. In the darkness, however, they sense that each one is still wide-awake and continue talking. The mother, in particular, speaks at length. She talks of the father, how he was, what he used to say, and what he did when the children, Guido and his sister, were young.

Without knowing the details, Guido has always been aware of a serious dissension between his mother and father involving the repeated, flagrant infidelities of the husband and the jealousy of the wife. Yet now all this seems blotted out in the memory of Guido's mother. The story of the marriage she tells now, the story of their life together, becomes an exemplary model for others to imitate. She describes the marriage in terms of eternal characteristics—births, domestic problems and joys, companionship, and reciprocal affection lasting all the life of both parties together. It is as if death had wiped out the dissension between them.

A silence in the darkness. Then the voice of the mother resumes. This time, she asks about Guido's wife. Why hasn't

Gianna come? What is she doing? Why have they no children? Are Guido and Gianna getting along well?

Guido gives vague answers. The mother, however, presses him. She insists on talking about Guido's wife, as if she had guessed some time ago the truth about their relationship. The mother speaks about her son's marriage with an earnestness she has never used before, perhaps because only now, with the death of her husband, does she feel a strong sense of the sacred and absolute value of the conjugal tie.

A profound uneasiness comes over Guido. His mother has always been a woman of few words. She has always shown a great deal of restraint about her children and their private affairs, a restraint that could have been construed as indifference or inability to understand. Now, however, this nocturnal outpouring, this solemn admonition, and this voice that seems, in the darkness, an echo of something eternal strike Guido with incredible force.

Guido does not take her questions as a gentle invitation to confess to her. He has no more intention of blurting out everything that has gone on between him and his wife than a criminal would have of confessing his crimes to the judge who interrogates him. Yet now, suddenly, his actions, his thoughts, his amusements, and his love affairs take on a new coloring for him—that of guilt, wrongdoing, and sin. This is a coloring that the death of his father and the words of his mother have created for him. Confronting this new vision of his life, Guido feels bewildered and dizzy.

Then in Guido's troubled mind, the image of Anita becomes superimposed on that of Gianna with a kind of innocent softness and naturalness. He is forced to ask himself somewhat fearfully what Anita represents to him and what place she has taken, or is taking, in his life. . . .

As dawn approaches, the mother drifts off to sleep. Guido, however, lies there with his eyes wandering over the objects of the room, the furniture, and the walls whose contours appear and disappear in the coming of the light of dawn. He looks at those things that offered themselves to his father's eyes and thoughts for so many years.

"Are you awake, Guido?"

The mother's sleep lasted roughly for half an hour. Not completely awake yet, she is still partially absorbed in a dream. She speaks as if she were just returning from a distant land. "I dreamed of papa," she says.

She remains silent for a few moments, perhaps to pursue the elusive apparition of the dead man with her partially awakened memory. "I dreamed," she continues after awhile, "that he was waking up . . . here . . . where you are. . . . He went to the mirror to put on his necktie and he looked at me. . . ."

The mother falls silent again. She struggles not to lose the precise memory of that look, which surprised her and moved her as if it were a revelation of something very important.

"He looked at me. . . . He seemed melancholy. . . . He looked at me with an expression of reproach . . . as if he wanted to tell me not to cry . . . not to be sad. . . ." She pauses, bewildered for a moment, and then continues, "Yes . . . reproach . . . but also regret. . . ." And finally she cries silently.

XXI

It is 10:30 on a burning hot, oppressive morning. Guido hurries to rejoin Anita at the small hotel. She has already come down and waits for him in the lobby. At once they leave the hotel and walk toward the beach.

They are at the outer end of the beach of Fano. Not many other people are present. Yet there is the kind of holiday or vacation atmosphere typical of seaside resorts. In the strong light, among the cries of children, Guido and Anita talk to each other. Both seem a little tired and somewhat dazed. Guido tells her the latest news from his home and relates what he has done and what he must do concerning his father's burial. Toward evening the

funeral people will transfer the body to the cathedral as is customary. This means that Guido will have to get his mother out of the
house so that she doesn't experience directly that terrible
moment of separation. Also Guido has had to take care of a
thousand things: the flowers, the inscription tablet on the tomb,
etc. Everywhere he went, he encountered old friends and
acquaintances. All of them were genuinely saddened by his
father's death. They said over and over like a refrain, "He was so
cheerful he made everyone else feel good." One of the women
working in the florist shop had red eyes from crying. Guido
thinks there must have been a relationship between his father
and this woman like the one between Anita and him. . . .

Guido explains that he must leave Anita to go back to the
house. Throughout the conversation, she has been extremely
sympathetic. She is secure in the role she has chosen. She
behaves like one of the family. "Have you eaten?" she asks in her
new, sad voice without a trace of exaggeration or pretense in it.
"How is your mother bearing up?" she adds. "Why don't you buy
her a rosary?"

Strangely moved and somewhat puzzled by Anita, Guido
says good-by and starts to leave. Anita's former liveliness
returns, although in a softer form. She doesn't want him to go so
soon. With an unconscious and unexpected surge of love, she
wants to stay with him a little longer, or at least to go with him
through the town on his round of errands. He is afraid of being
seen with her by his friends and relatives. Yet Anita insists. She
will walk behind him on the same street, but at a distance, pretending not to be with him. It would be boring for her to remain
alone another day in the little hotel.

XXII

Followed at a distance by Anita, Guido carries out his
errands in the festive streets of the town. She follows him up to
his house and waits outside while he goes in. She looks at the lit-

tle garden and the silent house, and she watches the comings and goings of some relatives.

At last Guido comes out again, this time with his mother, his sister, and his brother-in-law. Silent and self-absorbed, the mother passes Anita. Her children support her by the arms. The mother seems to have regressed to the state of a bewildered child. The family climbs into Guido's huge car and departs. Anita lingers where she is standing and watches the car disappear from sight.

Guido brings the family to a restaurant on the sea for dinner. Both he and his sister want to entertain their mother and draw her out of her depression. They try to engage her in conversation. The mother, however, does not want to go in the restaurant. "It's too expensive," she says with the ancient humility of poor women who have maintained a sad dignity throughout life. And after she decides to enter and eat on the bright sunny veranda, the mother speaks as if she were lost in the past, using the ancient language of mothers: "Chew your food carefully, Guido, or else you'll make yourself sick. . . . Do you remember, Guido, how much you liked mashed potatoes when you were little?"

XXIII

It is late when the family returns to the house. The father has already been transferred to the cathedral. A few relatives are in the house. For the first time the mother feels the full impact of the realization that her husband is gone forever and that she is now alone. She withdraws, shaking, into a frightening silence. The mother wanders through the house and goes into the room that contained her husband's body until recently. Falling on her knees by the empty bed, with her hands over her face, she moans. Then she begins to speak. Having followed her into the room, Guido goes close to her now and stands behind her. He hears the confused, senseless words his mother speaks in a hollow voice: "Have you left me? Have you left me like this? How could you ever do this to me?"

A few minutes later, the mother continues in a louder voice, which seems oddly calm now: "I thank you. . . . Giovanni, do you understand? We have nothing to complain about. . . . Our children have grown up . . . and have found their way. . . . They follow in our footsteps. . . ."

XXIV

At ten o'clock that night a celebration is taking place on the seafront street. Beneath the endless rows of sparkling streetlights, vacationers and young people from the town form a kind of parade. Some walk, others ride bicycles, and still others drive cars. They move forward amid shouting, laughter, and strains of popular music played by various orchestras. Far off along the coast, fireworks explode in the sky.

Through this street, Guido's Cadillac makes its way slowly. Guido is taking Anita to supper in a restaurant that seemed to him an almost mythical place when he was a child. He tells Anita about evenings when as a boy he wandered about in these streets with his young friends, admiring—almost venerating—the "gentlemen" who entered this restaurant. The place was a glittering symbol of luxury and wealth.

They arrive at the restaurant. It is at the end of a wharf. Now it seems a little weather-beaten. Certainly it is less grand than it was in Guido's memory. Only a few people are in the restaurant. A small orchestra is playing. Guido and Anita seek out a table apart from the others, looking out on the sea.

On the beach, in the white backwash of the waves, some fishermen are engaged in their toil. The evening is warm and calm. Guido seems to loosen up a bit in this atmosphere of peacefulness and well-being. He seems to lose his usual detached, ironic, and restrained manner. He confides in Anita. With sincerity and his usual bluntness, he tells her the long story of his relationship with his family. It is a story of a lack of understanding between father and son, begun in Guido's adolescence. Maybe it was like the usual lack of understanding between fathers and sons, but in the case of Guido and his father it was probably made more severe by the intensity of feeling on both sides. With the passing of months and years, the rift grew larger. When Guido was not quite seventeen, on bad terms with his family and fed up with life in a provincial town, he ran away, almost like a fugitive, to seek his fortune elsewhere. After that, for many years, the separation had been absolute. Then there was a kind of reconciliation, but it was only formal and superficial. After the war, Guido and his family saw each other two or three times at most.

Anita listens to all this carefully and sympathetically. Even though she excuses Guido and justifies his actions, it is clear, however, that she doesn't succeed in understanding one such as Guido. She is on the side of the family and familial love. These are the kinds of things that, she feels, give life its meaning and purpose.

XXV

Guido and Anita leave the restaurant and walk along the seafront street, which is almost empty by now. They come to a large building. Its walls and long rows of windows loom out of the darkness of the night. It is the elementary school that Guido attended as a child. The emotion of seeing it again breaks the last barrier in Guido restraining him from a complete opening up— to Anita and even to himself.

The death of his father and the return to his father's town have given Guido a revelation or a rediscovery. He does not know yet what he has learned; he knows only that he has learned something. The world he has relegated to the past, he sees now, is still living. It surrounds him. It is an old world, this world of his father's town, but it is an extraordinary and miraculously vital one. There is here an abundance of certain feelings that Guido had forgotten for a long time. The simple fullness of the emotions here and the security of a life both limited and profound strike him forcefully now at this time, when the kind of modern life he was living had begun to trouble him and throw him into a state of disillusion and anguish. He feels a strong urge to give up the struggle and return to the kind of life his father lived and the kind of life that had been mapped out for him.

Meanwhile, Guido and Anita walk on farther in the silent night. They have left the seafront, and, accompanied by the hollow rumble of the surf, they have plunged into the network of interior streets that lead toward the heart of the city. They come to a little photography store with sad, dusty, small display windows.

Guido pauses to look at some of the photographs on display. Some of them are very old. Amused and excited, Guido recognizes some of the people. . . . He sees Gradisca! His delight and excitement soar. The photograph, which must have been taken at least twenty years ago, shows a provocative, very beautiful young lady.

Guido tells Anita that Gradisca was well known in the town. In fact, she was the town's scandal. All the boys were crazy about her legendary breasts and sumptuous buttocks. An entire generation of secondary-school male students committed their first sins while thinking about her. It was said that one time a high-ranking person came to the town on official business and that this voluptuous, very beautiful woman was sent to him at night as a kind of homage. When she was alone with the official, she revealed her hidden treasures to him and bade him respectfully, "*Gradisca*," which means, "Please help yourself."

During the era of Gradisca's prime, Guido was a high-school student. He earned a little bit of pocket money by drawing caricatures of the actors in the movies at the Fulgor, and the owner of the movie house often let him in free of charge. One afternoon in the balcony, Guido found himself alone with Gradisca. It was like a dream. In his pocket Guido had no money at all, just two cigarettes. He began moving closer to her. And then, very slowly, as if there were people around him, he attempted. . . . But quickly and miraculously, as with the high-ranking official, she revealed her splendors to Guido, saying calmly and irritatedly, "Looking for something?"

The memory of this woman and this first encounter with love fills Guido with a sinister glee. He laughs and laughs.

Anita's alarm and concern over Guido's strange laughter make her all the more beautiful. Side by side, they resume their walk in the warm, empty night. Still caught up in his glee, Guido looks over Anita: her breasts, her hips, and her very light, summer dress. "Gradisca! Gradisca!" he cries at her, his eyes flashing. He has become excited by this fierce, childish game of make-believe he has hit upon.

Anita is bewildered. She is torn between embarrassment and real hurt. This usually submissive, soft woman wants to rebel against the tone of Guido's voice and this make-believe game he has invented, but she can only murmur, "Please don't say that."

Guido is seized with desire for Anita again. He embraces her, touches her, and squeezes her. A little bit frightened, she begs him, "Be good, Guido. . . . Come on, now. Be good."

She stops speaking. There is desperation in her eyes. But Guido continues. All the sensual, childish, and irrational aspects of his psyche have come to the surface, and they dominate him. The rational, intellectual components of his make-up have vanished. His love for Anita seems now to have come from this violent source.

XXVI

They resume walking, getting farther from the sea and closer to the interior of the city. They reach a large piazza, made more striking than usual by the darkness and the solitude. Here Guido stops again. A new emotion shakes him violently. A tablet on a wall gives the name of the piazza: "Square of the Martyrs."

Guido explains to Anita that three partisans had been killed here. The three were boys under twenty years of age. He had known them. For a few days, he had been with them in the mountains at Perticara. These were the days of the Resistance movement of World War II—days of great hopes. It seemed then that a new world might be born out of the days of blood and heroism. Everyone was caught up in that illusion, and everyone became a little bigger, better, and more generous as a result. And now . . . there is only the silence that weighs on the large square where the three martyred boys are a forgotten legend. . . .

A farmer on a bicycle pedals slowly and wearily across the piazza and then disappears like a phantom.

It is now dawn again. A gentle streak of light appears in the sky above the sea.

Guido and Anita move on, and then, as if by a miracle, they find themselves in front of the cathedral. The body of Guido's father has been brought here prior to the funeral service, which is to take place the next day. Guido is seized with a frenzied desire to see his father one last time. Nothing can deter him. He is like a headstrong child.

The main entrance and the side doors are locked. Guido, however, remembers that there is another way in, a secret one, which he has known about since childhood.

Along the sides of the fifteenth-century church there are five or six enormous windows with twisted Gothic columns and marble decoration. Affixed to the sills of the windows are some marble arks, which were intended as religious ornamentation but which, in fact, serve as roosts for pigeons and places where children play. These arks smell of dust, dried feathers, and the droppings of pigeons that have come there to die. Guido recalls that the last window toward the back has set into it a tiny door, which opens into the apse.

To get up to this window is very difficult. It requires a skilled climber who can use bricks that jut out and cornices to hoist himself up. Guido, however, won't listen to reason. He scrambles up the wall and perches on the window ledge. Poor Anita is forced to follow him in this foolhardy enterprise. She, too, scales the wall. Guido helps her and urges her on impatiently.

At last, they are together on the window ledge with the pigeon feathers and the droppings that litter the marble ark. And they discover that the tiny door has been walled up.

XXVII

After Guido gets over his initial feeling of disappointment, he becomes aware of the situation around him. The sky is whitening with infinite weariness. Anita is next to him in the solitude of a hiding place such as he might have picked in a child's game. The silence is profound.

Becoming feverishly excited again, Guido hugs Anita to him with a force that almost hurts her. His excess of emotion is by now so far beyond the usual bounds that Anita is overwhelmed completely. A kind of fear or grief appears in her eyes. Guido kisses her avidly and pours out his feelings to her. He loves her. Truly, he loves her, he declares excitedly, but also sincerely. If, after all, his return to this town and the death of his father have revealed anything to him, such as the continuing existence of an ancient world with its strongly felt emotions and its surety, it is Anita who brings this world to life and makes it vibrant for him. No one else except Anita can give him that sense of a full and secure life and that sense of profound serenity. For her, he is ready now to do anything—to leave his work, his wife, and Rome. He is ready now to begin all over again.

Trembling, Anita listens to Guido in silence and then collapses against him.

In that alcove for pigeons with its marble ornamentation, daylight enters. The roofs of the houses may now be seen clearly. In the distance we are able to make out the hills and the marina. We hear the voices of women. Some of them pass on bicycles, calling out, through the piazza before the cathedral. Then the silence of the dawn resumes.

XXVIII

In the splendor of the summer morning the funeral seems like a festival. A large crowd forms in front of the cathedral. A swarm of photographers have come down from Bologna. There is a band. And on the side streets around the cathedral, little boys jabber excitedly.

The people in the crowd jostle one another. They are dressed in black and look like merchants on market day. The crowd includes relatives, friends, acquaintances, and curious onlookers. These people press up the front steps to the cathedral.

Within the cathedral the atmosphere is chaotic. No one seems to be paying attention to the service. People move about. Children shuffle in and out of pews continuously. The brutal, screeching sound of the benches being pushed and moved fills the air. The noise is deafening.

The funeral service comes to an end, and the confusion at the moment of departure reaches a peak. As the coffin is being carried out of the cathedral, Guido's mother, who was so strong during the service and held in her pain so carefully, breaks down completely. She feels physically ill. Guido has to hold her up. Meanwhile, as if in a hallucination with the world reduced to fragments, Guido sees the coffin being carried out by the pallbearers with starts and stops over the heads of the crowd . . . and behind it the lines of orphans,[10] the nuns, and the friends.

XXIX

Outside, the air is warm and extremely soft. The horses that will draw the hearse paw the ground almost joyfully. The bells ring out with a sound that seems close to cheerfulness. The band plays very softly. And then the funeral cortege begins to move.

The funeral procession passes slowly along the main street full of silent people. As the cortege advances, the people in their homes on the street close their shutters.[11]

---

[10] It was formerly the custom to use the children in orphanages run by the church as part of funeral corteges.

[11] Another funeral custom. The homeowner's act of closing his shutters is a way of participating in the grief of the occasion, and it is an act of respect for the family of the deceased. Along the same lines, a shopkeeper might choose to close his door and suspend business operations while the cortege passes.

Supporting his mother on his arm, Guido walks behind the hearse as if he were in a dream. He looks around, disturbed by elements of a reality that ought to be terrible, but that are soft and gentle instead. Among the crowd he sees a middle-aged woman crying. Her face is hidden by the black handkerchief she wears on her head, according to the custom of women in provincial towns. Guido believes that she must have been another love in his father's life like the saleswoman in the florist shop Guido encountered earlier. And then a little farther on, he sees Anita and finds that she resembles that woman, although Anita is younger and more attractive. Anita is similar in the pose she strikes, in her gestures, in the handkerchief on the top of her head, and in her crying.

Guido goes on foot to the Ponte della Marecchia and then drives his car from there to the cemetery, which is located in the fields along the road to Rome.

XXX

The next morning Guido gets up early to depart. He has a long trip before him. The good-bys are brief. By now everything is concluded. His mother and sister accompany Guido into the garden in front of the house and watch him drive off.

XXXI

In the small hotel by the sea there is a curious mood of silence, emptiness, and abandonment. As with the funeral, everything here seems concluded, too. Perhaps this is the way things are at the hotel so early in the morning. The vacationers are sleeping, and things have not come to life yet in the hotel.

Somewhat uneasy, Guido gets out of the car and runs into the hotel. The lobby is empty. In the small dining room a waitress is setting places for breakfast. The atmosphere is drowsy. Two little boys descend the stairs excitedly with their sailboats and sandpails, and Guido rushes up the stairs past them.

The door to Anita's room is open. The room itself is empty. The bed is unmade. Bewildered, Guido looks around. All the luggage is gone. There is no sign of Anita.

Caught in the throes of a kind of terror, Guido wheels around and starts for the door. Just then a chambermaid appears in the doorway in front of him. A little bit frightened by Guido's expression, she holds out an envelope to him. "The young lady left this for you," she tells Guido.

It is a short, hastily written letter. "Dear Guido, you are the only man I love. Please believe that is true. I swear it to you. But I think our love won't work. It is better this way. I would have preferred to tell you this face to face, but who could ever win an argument with you? You would have persuaded me to stay with you for better or worse. So I am slipping away without seeing you. I love you so much, your Anita."

Guido feels at a loss. Hurt and blind rage overcome him. He doesn't know what to do or where to go. The loss of Anita is like a death for Guido. He slams the door shut. Alone in the room, he rereads the letter. Then he crumples it up and throws it away. Uncontrollable tears well up in him from deep in his being. He falls on his knees by Anita's bed. In a kind of hysteria he rocks back and forth, alternating insults of Anita with appeals to her amid his groans. He is reduced to a quivering, shapeless mass of desperation.

XXXII

It is now midmorning. The sun is sparkling merrily. The beach is full of people clamoring loudly.

Weighed down as if by age, Guido gets listlessly into his car. He starts it up and heads off on the road to Rome. He drives slowly, almost at the pace of a man on foot, and steers mechanically with his mind off in the distance.

The small hotel, the seaside road, the beach, and the town itself are behind Guido now. It seems clear that he will never return. At the Ponte della Marecchia, the town can be seen in the distance in the serenity of the morning light.

In front of Guido is the cemetery. Guido drives toward it, still moving slowly. At the gate, he makes a sudden decision and brakes the car abruptly.

Guido enters the cemetery. The sunlight is strong and cheerful. Because it is the middle of summer, the flowers and the grass have grown high and cover some of the marble monuments and tombs. In a corner of the cemetery undergoing repairs, some bricklayers with white paper hats are working so cheerfully that they look like they might break into song at any moment.

Guido moves farther into the cemetery toward the corner where the tomb of his father lies. He sees, however, that someone is at the tomb. Kneeling by it is the figure of a woman. With amazement and joy, Guido recognizes her. It is Anita! Her back is turned to him. Gaining control of himself, Guido moves up to her slowly. Along the side of the road is a railroad track, and the din of a passing train covers the sound of his footsteps.

Anita is bent over the tomb of Guido's father. The tablet on the tomb shows the name and a photograph of the man.[12] In the photograph the father is smiling and appears somewhat overbearing.

Guido hesitates to disturb Anita. Only after some time has passed does he call to her.

Her first reaction is one of fear. Then she turns to him a face stained with tears. Overcoming her surprise at his presence, she smiles, dries her tears, and says hello.

With great control, they speak to each other gently and amicably as if nothing painful had happened between them. The life and beauty in Anita seem to burst out of her as they had done before.

---

[12] It is typical even today for the family to put a photograph of the deceased on the tablet. The photograph is protected by a glass or plastic covering and usually shows the dead person in his prime or as the family would like him to be remembered.

Anita is unshakable in her determination to leave Guido, but now that chance and piety have brought them together again they can explain their feelings to each other. Anita gives Guido her reasons as best she can. Her simple and inexact words, however, are less important than the truth that lies behind them.

Facing this truth, Guido has to give in. He is beaten. And yet he is also victorious in a sense. The love that binds him to Anita is not just an explosive, sensual outpouring. There is something more profound, more valuable, in the love. This something is his rediscovery of life in its simplicity and fullness. In Anita, Guido finds the same kind of life that he rediscovered in the events surrounding his father's death in the old province where Guido was born. But Guido's discovery in both cases must be sterile in a way. He has no illusions about this. Guido has a marital commitment that he cannot throw over for Anita, just as he has a world of culture, art, consciousness, and even anguish that he can't abandon for a world, however marvelous, that must now be left behind.

In the distance the noon bells ring cheerfully. A skylark drifts down toward Guido and Anita in a meandering flight, singing happily, and then climbs away through the luminous air. Guido and Anita walk out of this cemetery full of light and pleasant odors. It is the moment of good-by.

With a painful effort Guido gets into his car and drives off. The image of Anita waving good-by, however, is so gentle and loving that his sadness is not without a shimmer of joy.

APPENDIX

Fellini's Later Uses of Material from the Two Screenplays

Moraldo in the City	Later Work
1. The general situation of the young man from the provinces attempting to succeed in the city.	1. *Roma* (1972). This situation provides one of several themes in this film. Fellini details his young hero's first day in Rome, as he, like Moraldo, sets out to test himself in the city.
2. Section X. Using a sketch by Lange as a model, Moraldo attempts to paint an advertisement on a shoemaker's window but botches the job and is humiliated.	2. "Via Veneto: Dolce Vita" (1962). Although Fellini does not use this episode in any of his completed films, he does relate it as an autobiographical event in this essay on his adventures on the Via Veneto. Lange's equivalent in the essay is the illustrator Rinaldo Geleng.
3. Section XXXIV. The visit of Moraldo's father to the city and the depiction of a failed attempt by the father to bridge the gap between father and son. The father invites the son to return, but Moraldo declines, and the father departs the next morning.	3. *La Dolce Vita* (1960). The father visits Marcello in the city. They go together to the Kit Kat Club, and later the father suffers a mild heart attack in a female dancer's room. Embarrassed in front of his son, the father departs the next morning, despite Marcello's entreaties that he stay so they can talk with each other.
4. Section XXXVII. The ending of the screenplay, where Moraldo walks back to the center of town as the lights of evening come on. He is cheered by the movement of people around	4. *Nights of Cabiria* (1956). The ending consists of Cabiria's walk back to town in the evening after she had been rejected and robbed by her fiancé. She is cheered by a group of young

him. These people include a girl who smiles, a boy who rides a bicycle and whistles, and a pair of lovers.

people who overtake her. They play musical instruments. A pair of lovers ride a Vespa. A girl bids Cabiria, "Good evening."

Il Bidone (1955). A negative version. The dying swindler attempts to call out to a group of women and children walking on a country road. The group does not hear him, however, and passes him by.

8½ (1963). Perhaps a stylized version of the ending. Guido attempts to direct and then joins a moving circle of people from his life.

A Journey with Anita

1. Section VII. Guido and Anita visit the town abandoned for more than three hundred years and make love.

2. Section IX. Partially intoxicated, Anita does an energetic and sexual dance at the farmhouse. Guido fails to keep up with her and does a pratfall.

3. Section XI. Angry about Anita's behavior with the workers, Guido attacks her verbally and then forces her from his car. Later he returns to find her seated on a wall, filing her nails.

Later Work

1. *La Dolce Vita*. Marcello and the party-goers visit the deserted Renaissance villa at Bassano di Sutri, and Marcello makes love to Jane, the American painter, in an empty room.

2. *La Dolce Vita*. In the nightclub in the Baths of Caracalla, Sylvia abandons Marcello as a dance partner and breaks into an exhibitionistic and energetic dance with the actor Frankie Stout, who looks like a satyr.

3. *La Dolce Vita*. In a parked car outside of Rome, Marcello argues angrily with his mistress Emma about her possessive, maternal love. She leaves the car, gets back in, and then is put out by Marcello. He drives off but returns at daybreak to discover her pacing back and forth with a bunch of flowers she has gathered.

4. Section XV. The mysteriously prompt arrival of relatives and friends after the death of Guido's father. Guido can barely remember some of the relatives.

4. *Amarcord* (1974). The equally prompt arrival of relatives and friends in the morning serves to let Titta know that his mother has died during the night. Titta also has difficulty recognizing some of the people who crowd into the house.

5. Section XIX. Eugenio's elaborate plan for the tomb of Guido's father. Since the tomb described in the last scene of the screenplay seems more modest, we may assume Guido rejected Eugenio's plan.

5. *8½*. In a fantasy the ghost of Guido's father returns to criticize his son for giving him a tomb that is too small.

6. Section XX. Guido spends the night in his father's place in the parents' double bed with his mother, suggesting Oedipal wish-fulfillment.

6. *8½*. In a fantasy Guido ushers his father into his tomb and then kisses his mother passionately, also suggesting Oedipal wish-fulfillment.

Roma. A sunburnt son curls up in bed with his enormous mother before the eyes of the young protagonist on his first day in Rome, giving a comic version of the Oedipal situation.

7. Section XXIV. Guido's memory of the restaurant by the sea, which seemed to him to be a glittering spot of luxury and wealth.

7. *Amarcord*. The presentation of the Grand Hotel, especially the scene in which Titta and his friends watch the older males in white dinner jackets romance the female tourists on the hotel's veranda.

"My Rimini" (1967). The dances on the terraces of the elegant Grand Hotel of Rimini are described in this autobiographical essay.

8. Section XXV. Guido's account of how Gradisca, the town vamp, got her name by inviting a visiting official, "Please help yourself."

8. *Amarcord*. The lawyer recounts the same myth as an example of one of the fabulous events that occurred in the Grand Hotel. The story is shown on screen.

"My Rimini." The story is recounted here as part of the lore about Rimini.

9. Section XXV. Guido's account of the time he moved close to Gradisca in the empty movie theater, attempted a sexual overture, and was casually dismissed.

9. *Amarcord*. Titta's flashback confession of the same scene in the movie theater with Gradisca. He fondles her thigh and is again rebuffed casually by the more experienced woman.

"My Rimini." Fellini tells the story as an experience in his adolescence.

10. Sections XXVIII and XXIX. The funeral service in the church for Guido's father is marred by the comings and goings of the people and the screeching of benches. Then the funeral cortege moves through town in inappropriately splendid weather.

10. *Amarcord*. The more solemn funeral service for Titta's mother is spoiled by the fainting of Titta's uncle. Then the funeral cortege moves through town on a bright day, which we learn is the first day of spring.

11. Section XXXII. The gentle and loving image of Anita waving good-by to Guido seems to sum up a simple, attractive life he leaves as he returns to Rome.

11. *La Dolce Vita*. The close-ups of Paola, the young girl from Umbria, as she smiles sadly and waves good-by to Marcello as he rejoins his friends from Rome at the end of the film. She, too, seems an image of a simple and attractive life left behind.